"No!" Travis screamed as he flailed at the water. "Nooooooo!"

But it was too late, for the stick suddenly descended and with a sodden thud smashed against the body of the goose. Chester jerked, released Alec's ear, and rolled onto his side. The stick was in the air and descending once more when Travis, finally on the bank, dived beneath it and covered the goose with his body.

Whump! The heavy stick jarred against his ribs, smashing at his wind, and Travis blanched with the pain.

"Kill it!" one or two kids were shouting as hands tugged to pull Chester away from the boy. "Get the kid out of the way and kill that crazy bird!"

Travis, too sore and winded to cry out, clung fiercely to his pet, doing his best to shield it from further blows. But there were too many hands, he could feel the goose slipping away, and he was powerless to prevent the attack.

D1301675

THE THANKSGIVING PROMISE

BLAINE AND BRENTON YORGASON

TOR

A TOM DOHERTY ASSOCIATES BOOK

This is a work of fiction. All the characters and events portrayed in this book are fictional, and any resemblance to real people or incidents is purely coincidental.

THE THANKSGIVING PROMISE

Copyright © 1986 by Blaine and Brenton Yorgason

Cover photograph copyright © 1986 The Walt Disney Company

All rights reserved, including the right to reproduce this book or portions thereof in any form.

First Tor printing: November 1986

A TOR Book

Published by Tom Doherty Associates, Inc.
49 West 24 Street
New York, N.Y. 10010

ISBN: 0-812-59053-8
CAN. ED.: 0-812-59054-6

Printed in the United States of America

0 9 8 7 6 5 4 3 2 1

For all who read this
may you each
recognize
your own great
worth.

Acknowledgments

For help with this story we owe thanks to our children, who made excellent models; and to Mel Ferrer and Walt Disney Pictures, who made the filming possible.

MY BROTHER

There was a time long years ago
when I would gaze longingly up
into the unseeing eyes of
my brother.
I did this often, hoping somehow that
he would hear my silent cries and
want to be my friend.

Those days are gone now,
yet they linger,
floating in the memories of
my youth.
One day especially
drifts by often—
perhaps for us the beginning.

As boys we were set on learning,
artistic adventure stirred our hearts,
over a fire in the orchard,
melting crayons for a
waxen sculpture.
Fascinated, I, the younger,
hoisted bravely the container.

Stumbling, then, too near the fire,
molten wax spraying and searing,
my torso now engulfed in pain.
Terror-filled I fled unseeing,
racing to nowhere,
hurting—
dying—

Suddenly I was beneath my brother
who recklessly beat out the flames.
Something happened that
heat-filled morning,
an investment made with pain and
love, searing deeply,
finally melting heart to heart.

And so, reflecting, words now tumble
midst the tears such memories bring.
Crayons of a different sort we
melt now
in the orchards of our lives,
sculpting, lifting, pressing onward,
because forever we are brothers.

—Brenton G. Yorgason

Contents

INTRODUCTION

"Shhhhhh!"

The early morning silence was broken by the repeated warning of silence. Off in the east the sky was graying noticeably, and in the marshes along Chester Cove, the wildlife was already singing the songs of a new day.

Yet to the four teenage boys who crept forward through the bulrushes and cattails, the beauty of the morning was nonexistent. The boys were hunting, and the alcohol they had consumed throughout the night had done nothing to enhance their skills.

"Burrrrpp!" one of the boys suddenly belched.

"Shut up," Alec Suggins, the obvious leader, snarled. "You want to scare the bir . . . ds . . . ?"

"Har-de-har-har," the boy called Jess laughed quietly. "Alec, you're worse than Tommy."

"Oh, yeah? Says who, you little jerk?"

"Uh . . . uh . . . I'm sorry, Alec. I didn't mean it."

"You better not have, pip-squeak," Alec declared. "Now, are we going hunting, or are you guys going to sit here and belch all day long?"

Silently the three others dropped their eyes, and so without another word, Alec turned and quietly pushed his way through the undergrowth.

Overhead, a "V" of Canadian geese passed, their honkings loud in the early morning air. Alec, pausing to look up, pointed excitedly as the flock broke formation and dropped toward the still-unseen cove.

"Did you see those?" he whispered. "Honkers! Ol' Betsy here is going to bring a few of them down in about three minutes."

"Yeah," the one called Tommy agreed. "My dad's shotgun has never missed. I'll be getting a few, too."

"The reason that gun's never missed," Alec whispered, grinning, "is you've never been shooting it. I'll bet five dollars you don't hit anything but water."

"Five dollars?" Jess gasped.

"Yeah. Five dollars says none of you'll hit anything but air. I've never seen guys get so corked up on three six-packs."

"Now, come on," Alec concluded, motioning the boys forward with his shotgun. "We've got some birds to kill."

Moments later there was a whispered "Fire!" from Alec, followed by a thunderous explosion as four shotguns fired at once. Flocks of terrified geese scattered wildly in the air while several fluttered wounded into the bulrushes or lay still upon the water.

There was a moment of stunned silence in the Cove, and then, as one, the four boys rose to their feet, shouting exuberantly at their success.

"Look at that big ol' sucker," Jess shouted. "I nailed 'im right in the head."

"The heck you did," Tommy argued. "I got that one first shot."

Alec, disgusted with the bickering of his friends and nervous because of the approaching daylight, cut them off in the middle of their argument.

"Look, you creeps, I killed the big one. Now, come on. Let's get out of here before someone comes."

The three other boys, each as nervous as Alec, lowered their guns and began looking furtively around.

"Do you see anybody, Alec?" Jess whispered.

"No, but we made a lot of noise, and I think we had better scram."

"Me, too," Tommy whispered as he threw his cigarette into the grass. "Let's get back to your convertible, Alec. If I'm picked up once more by that clown who calls himself a game warden, I'm dead meat."

"You are anyway, sucker." Alec laughed. "Come on, you guys. Let's go."

Quickly the boys made their way to Alec Suggins's bright red convertible, climbed in, and with squealing tires sped away. And not one of them noticed the small yet growing circle of fire that the cigarette had started.

MAY

Chapter 1
Coach and Alec

"Did you find him?"

The whispered question hung suspended in the stillness of the morning. The air, heavy with the sweet smell of spring, was almost electric with tension, and Jason Tilby shuffled his feet nervously. Finally, though, when there was no response, he turned his head slightly so he could better see his younger brother, and then urgently whispered his question once more.

"Steve, did you *find* him?"

His face a study in concentration, Steven Tilby stared straight ahead, his eyes never leaving the face of Coach Gruninger. His head, however, nodded slightly, almost imperceptibly, and Jason breathed a sigh of relief.

"Good," he whispered. "Where is he?"

"Old Lady Anderson caught us," Steve hissed, still without turning his head. "She made him go stand with his class, and told me that if I made another sound she'd see that I flunked. She acts like she's still my teacher!"

"The old biddy," Jason snarled angrily. "Doesn't she see that he needs us? All those creeps in her class make fun of him."

"Who doesn't?"

"Well, it's not right. Just 'cause he's little and wears glasses and can't—"

"Sshhhh," Steve whispered quickly. "Coach is looking."

Jason lifted his eyes and stared into the face of Coach Gruninger, a bull of a man who thought much of himself and who was not actually a coach at all but simply a onetime substitute P.E. teacher who had somehow taken root and flourished. Still, he liked to be called Coach, and so everyone did. No one, no one *ever*, argued with Coach.

Again Jason's thoughts drifted to his youngest brother, and he found himself worrying, really worrying. In fact, he'd been worrying ever since his parents had asked him to watch out for Travis.

He'd hated the idea of that assignment, for kids laughed at Travis, and he couldn't bear being laughed at, too. Steve felt the same, and they'd only started walking with Trav and trying to be his friend because of what his dad had said he'd do if they didn't. But then one day a couple of kids had made fun of him as well as of Trav and then had taken off. He was powerless to do a whole lot about it because he couldn't catch them, and suddenly the whole thing had come home. From that moment Jason knew how Travis felt.

Since then he'd done his best to be not only Trav's friend but his bodyguard as well. Steve had tried, too, a little. But Jason knew that Steve's heart wasn't in it yet. Maybe in time, though, after Trav had come around a little . . .

The real trouble, however, was that Trav was stubborn and wanted no help. He was also a loner in some ways, and the fact that he was not very athletic didn't help much, either. He was sort of different from most of the other kids, including him and Steve. Travis seemed to think different kinds of thoughts, he liked to read and draw more than anything else, and he just didn't have many friends. And besides all that, he was still a little kid, and Jason was finding it harder and harder just carrying on a conversation with him.

Today was another problem, too. It was the school's annual Field Day, and Travis had no desire to be in attendance. But his grade depended not only upon his attendance but upon his participation. And so far he'd tried, he really had. But in his first race he'd fallen, and some of the kids, led especially by that creep Alec Suggins, had laughed, and Trav had taken off running. Steve had finally found him, but Old Lady Anderson wouldn't let them stand together, the next event was Trav's worst, and Coach wouldn't let up for anything.

Without wanting to at all, Jason shifted his eyes until he could see Alec, who was standing across the circle of kids and near the front by Coach. Alec Suggins was tall, a little taller than Jason, even. He was bronzed and muscular—the school jock— though Jason could actually beat him in several events. Worst of all, though, was the fact that Alec had a red convertible. Nobody else in the whole school had a car, let alone a convertible, for most of the kids were not quite old enough. But Alec was, having been held back or something in first grade, and now he used his age and strength to great advantage.

Grimly Jason stared at Alec, willing his eyes to remain on the older boy, not wanting them to shift, not wanting them to—

But then they did, despite his efforts otherwise, and Jason found himself glancing at the girl who stood next to Alec. However, he didn't look very long before his eyes darted away and his face started getting red. He was embarrassed even looking at her, though for the life of him he didn't know why. Of course it wasn't necessary that he watch her very long, anyway. Her picture, her image, was memorized in his mind, her blue-green eyes, her honey-blond hair, her upturned nose, her smiling mouth, everything. In fact, every time he closed his eyes she was all he could see. Yes, sir, without a doubt Sheryl Hanson was the cutest girl Jason had ever seen. And sadly, even tragically in his opinion, she was Alec Suggins's girlfriend.

"Dumb girl," he muttered to himself as he looked back at Alec, who was grinning at Coach. "How can she stand to like that creep? Why does a car have to be such a big deal to a girl? Wish I had the nerve to talk to her, to say something funny and make her laugh. She's got the happiest laugh I ever heard. Wouldn't do any good, though. She's

Alec's girl, the dumb thing. But maybe, maybe if I could save my money and get a car, then . . ."

"Jase, sssshhhh," Steve hissed. "Everybody can hear you talking to yourself."

More embarrassed than ever, Jason glanced at Steve, who was still staring at Coach. Darting his eyes, Jason looked at the kids around him, and when he saw a few snickers and knowing grins, his ears started to burn and he found himself wishing that he had died. Only he hadn't, and—

"All right," Coach suddenly bellowed into the silence, "listen up! All of you! We won't proceed until all I can hear is your hot and heavy breathing."

As Coach waited, Jason unobtrusively cast his eyes about until he finally saw his youngest brother. Travis was standing at the rear of the crowd, trying his best to look even smaller than he already was. If only Old Lady Anderson hadn't—

"That's better. Now, this is the rope climb, the last event before lunch. All of you know why. Twenty-five feet is a long way to pull yourself up with a gut full of food. Fat guts also make a bigger splat if you fall."

Coach listened gleefully to the chorus of groans and moans, winked at the loudly laughing Alec, and when the noise subsided, he continued.

"All year we've been practicing this climb, and some of you've developed real skill. A few of you are even approaching the school record, and with a little more work and a little more competitive spirit you just might break it. Alec here could do it today, and maybe he will."

Alec grinned widely, and Jason groaned inwardly

as he saw how Sheryl looked up at him. "Scrud," he snorted with disgust. "Cow eyes, just like Gerty's. What's the matter with her that—"

"However," Coach continued, "there is one among you whose ability puts him in a class all by himself, whose sense of competition can be compared to no one else's. I have decided to let him go first."

Eyes suddenly turned to Jason, and he ducked his head in alarm. It couldn't be him. Sure he could climb it, and pretty fast, too. Faster even than Alec. But not—

"Never in all my years of teaching," Coach continued, "have I worked with a boy like this one. He's been a real eye-opener for me, and I want you to learn from him, too. Travis Tilby, front and center, on the double!"

There were gasps from every direction, and Jason felt a sense of horror. Not Travis! Surely not Travis. He couldn't get more than six feet in the air. What was Coach . . . ?

The gasps had now turned to snickers, and Jason was suddenly aware that Steve was gripping his arm, pointing. Jason looked, and saw that the kids were pushing Travis forward, laughing as they did it, ignoring the look of terror on the boy's face. Jason thought of pushing forward himself and stopping it, but he didn't know exactly how to do it, and then Travis was standing before Coach, and the moment when he might have done something was forever past.

"Kids," Coach bellowed, his voice deep and manly, "you all know Travis, so I won't take time for formal introductions."

11

The crowd howled with laughter, and Jason stared at Alec's grinning face, sick at heart. But maybe, he suddenly thought, maybe . . .

"All year I've watched this boy," Coach went on, "and he has developed, almost in spite of the things I've tried to teach him, a system and style all his own. His sense of competition is unique, for he has none, and his abilities seem to match it. That's why I've chosen him to go first."

Jason's spirits dropped lower. It was bad enough when kids picked on Trav, but when grown-up adults started in on him . . .

"Now, young people," Coach continued, "I want each of you to watch this young man closely . . ."

Jason strained to see his brother, and felt Steve straining at his side. The air was again quiet, for no one was talking, no one was moving. Everyone was expectant, waiting.

". . . because," concluded Alec in his laughing voice, interrupting whatever it was that Coach had intended to say, "Travis 'The Wimp' Tilby is now going to show all of us how *not* to climb a rope!"

Jason's breath exploded outward much as though someone had slugged him. The world was filled with the roar of laughter, and he found himself straining to see Travis, aching to find his younger brother and tell him that it hadn't happened, wanting with all his heart to beat Alec into the ground, feeling as though Coach had mocked him personally instead of Travis by not stopping it. Then he realized that more than anything else he was hurting for his little brother, and he wanted suddenly to go to him, to find him, to teach him to climb the rope, to work with him until Trav could go up it faster than anyone else in the school. Then Trav could do it and they could shove the dang rope into Coach's and Alex's faces and—

Jason turned to Steve, realized that his brother had disappeared, and only then heard the voice coming from behind him, a voice filled with anger and disgust.

". . . that low-down miserable bully! And Coach! Who does he think he is, treating one of my boys . . ."

Jason spun around, and to his surprise found himself facing Old Lady Anderson.

"The big blow-hards," she muttered, her eyes snapping fire, "I . . . I ought to bust both of them right in the mouth! They're both babies. Jason, go take care of Travis now! *I'll* take care of Coach and Alec!"

And then, while Jason stared in amazement, Old Lady Anderson picked up her umbrella, held it before her like a spear, and began pushing her way forward through the crowd, her goal the hulking and loudly laughing forms of Coach and Alec Suggins.

Jason turned and ran, and as he ran his thoughts were filled with concern about why a cute sweet girl like Sheryl could like a rotten barf-bag like Alec and with ideas about how to help Trav get even. There would be a way, and he knew it. There always was. Only—

13

JUNE

Chapter 2
Competition vs. Opposition

Chester came into Travis's life in the back of Old Mr. Larson's pickup, and he was very nearly dead when he got there. He was in a box, the box was on top of a barrel, and even with those precautions one of the bummer lambs had jumped up and come mighty near to crushing him. That was probably why, when Travis saw the little creature, and saw what terrible condition it was in, the boy's heart opened up and Chester instantly moved in. At that time in his life, you see, Travis felt pretty close to anything that had been somewhat knocked about.

Chester had another problem too, a small problem which became evident only after Trav removed him from the box and snuggled him into his arms. Somewhere, somehow or other, Chester had lost one of his black webbed feet, and he was doomed to spend the rest of his life getting on as best he could

16

without it. When Trav saw that, his heart opened even further, and as he hurriedly wiped his sleeve across his eyes he knew more than ever that he and the baby goose he held in his arms were going to be good friends.

But listen to me! Here I am getting way out ahead of myself, and what kind of way is that to tell a decent story? Why, at the point in time when I want to start, Trav was still standing off by himself behind the black walnut tree, the Sanpete sky was still clouded over with his own personal brand of thirteen-year-old seventh-going-on-eighth-grade misery, the driveway dust was still calm and serene, and wealthy old Mr. Larson's new pickup was still only a period at the far end of the horizon, not yet even seen.

You see, Trav had no earthly idea that a baby Canadian honker goose named Chester was about to enter his life. Thing is, it was, and Trav, like it or not, would never be the same again. Nor would his family, for that matter. Why, you ask. Well, because that Chester-goose was a miracle worker of sorts, and that's what this story is going to be all about. Miracles.

But like I said, I'm getting somewhat ahead of myself, and I'd better retreat. At the moment I want to speak of, Jase and Steve Tilby, Travis's older brothers, were just finishing off a couple of healthy slices of watermelon. Jenni, Travis's younger sister, was right in the middle of her slice. Hank, his father, was still weeding in the garden, and Lois, his mother, was just looking around for her missing third son.

17

"Know what?" Steve was saying to no one in particular. "If I ever make a world, watermelons are going to be the only weeds on it, and they'll grow everywhere. I love 'em!"

"Me, too," Jenni replied quickly. "Watermelon weeds and bubble-gum weeds!"

"You can't grow bubble gum," Steve snorted with disgust.

"I can, too!"

"Stupid girl!"

"Mommy," Jenni wailed. "Steve called me—"

"Hush, you two," Lois interceded. "You'll never get any watermelon *or* bubble gum if you can't learn to be nice to each other."

"But, Mom," Steve argued, "she said—"

"Steve, I said stop."

"But you can't grow bubble gum . . ."

"Steven, I mean it! Stop arguing! Now, apologize to each other, both of you."

When they had, Lois turned toward the garden and so did not see the face her daughter pulled at Steve. Nor, for that matter, did she see her son's response. Or at least she didn't act like she had seen them. But then Lois Tilby was a canny woman, and she knew when to ignore and when not to. At that moment, obviously, she ignored.

"Hank, sweetheart," she asked, speaking as though nothing at all had happened between the two children, "have you seen Travis?"

Hank Tilby, who was just finishing the last row of corn, stopped, mopped his brow, and looked around.

"Nope," he replied quietly. "Last time I saw

18

him he was over in the carrots. Jase, did you see where he went?"

Jason, fifteen and finally going into high school, looked up from his watermelon and nodded. "He finally finished the carrots, I guess. Took him forever, though. Last I saw him he was running into the orchard."

"Without his watermelon?" Lois asked in surprise. "Jason, is something wrong?"

Jason looked quickly at Steve, who shrugged as if to say that whatever happened next was Jase's decision, and then he dropped his gaze. Jase did likewise, but his mother, pretty adept at reading signals among her children, pressed on.

"Jason," she said urgently, "something else has happened to Travis, hasn't it? If it's the boys on that team again, I'll . . ."

"It wasn't them, Mom. It was Coach. Coach and Alec Suggins."

"Coach? Alec? But I don't . . . Wait a minute. Field Day?"

Jason nodded, and Lois Tilby sat down quickly beside him, her face strained. Hank Tilby, seeing his wife's expression, strode over, sat down across the table from his eldest son, and asked him to begin. Jason did, and quickly the story of the rope climb unfolded.

"Oh," Lois cried when Jason finished, "poor Travis! What can we do to help him understand . . ."

"Travis doesn't need to understand," Jason shouted angrily. "It ain't him that's the problem. It's Alec, and Coach, too, I guess. Somebody ought to murder those big creeps!"

19

"Jason," his father responded, "let's hear no more of that sort of talk. People like that need to be pitied, and nothing else. Now, relax, Lois. I'll find Travis and talk to him. He simply needs to learn how to deal with this kind of thing. I just hope . . ."

And with those words Hank Tilby rose and walked quickly into the orchard. As he searched for his son, he thought of his own career as a salesman, and of the fierce competition that existed everywhere, competition that people needed to learn to face. He'd had to, and he was surviving economically because of it. Travis, he felt, was buckling under to pressures that he needed to learn to face, pressures of competition, and Hank felt that he needed to point that out to his son. He would, too, but gently, gently.

When at last he found the boy, he sat down beside him in the grass, and for long moments the two sat silently together.

"Jason told us about yesterday," he finally said to the boy. "Travis, I'm sorry that Coach Gruninger did that, and . . ."

"It wasn't Coach's fault," Travis replied quietly.

"What? But I thought . . ."

"It's my fault, Dad. Just like always. I'm the one who isn't any good at anything. I don't blame the kids for making fun of me. Or Coach, either. I can't play ball, climb the rope, or do anything the other guys do."

"It was probably just the pressure of the crowd," Hank said easily. "Why, I'll bet that if you were alone, you could . . ."

"I was alone last night," Travis replied bitterly.

"I went back to school after everyone had gone, and I did everything I could. I still didn't get past six or seven feet on that stupid rope. It's no good, Dad. I hate sports, and I mean it! Maybe that makes me weird, but I still do!"

Thoroughly taken aback by his son's statement, Hank turned to look at the boy. Why, he'd had no idea that Travis felt that way, and he was almost speechless with surprise.

"Trav," he responded finally, "just because you don't enjoy some sports doesn't make you weird."

"Some," Travis declared, his voice shaking with emotion. "Dad, I hate *all* of them. And I hate school and church, too! And sometimes I hate it here at home!"

Too astonished to be hurt or defensive, Hank stared at his youngest son. "But *why*?" he finally asked.

"Because everybody's always making everything into a contest where somebody has to win, like you did with weeding the garden today. And I hate 'em because I can't win. I always *lose*!"

"But, Trav, that isn't so. There aren't *that* many contests."

"Oh, yeah? Getting good grades on that dumb curve the teachers use for grading is a contest, reading the most books or writing the most pages in school is a contest, finding Scriptures in church is a contest, playing ball, racing cars in the pinewood derby in Cub Scouts, *everything*! They're all contests! And I hate them because I always *lose*!

"Coach says competition is the American way. It's what makes real men. He says it just like you

21

do when you talk about your job. Dad, I hate it, and I don't care if I ain't never going to be a real man. I don't like contests, I'll always be a loser, and I don't even want to be an American if that's what I have to do!"

For a long moment Travis was silent, his anger nearly spent and his confusion finally showing itself to his father.

"Dad, why is winning always so doggone important? Even that missionary in church last week told about baptizing the most people and winning contests. Dad, if I have to do that, then I . . . I don't ever want to be a m-missionary! I . . ."

And with that stammering statement the held-back tears finally came, and Travis sat shaking and sobbing next to his father.

Hank, deeply moved by his son's pain, put his arms around the boy and held him close. Then he silently prayed that he might have the wisdom to somehow lift the soul of his boy to the elevated place where God had originally placed it. And as he prayed, he found himself thinking of the contests he had himself created within his family, competition in such diverse things as learning poems and weeding the garden, competition which created losers as well as winners, competition which he had always thought of as good but which had so painfully injured his youngest son.

And suddenly Hank Tilby remembered. He remembered and finally understood a little thing he had heard and then forgotten, and he knew then what he had to tell his son. If only he could find the right way to do it.

For a few moments the two sat in silence, Hank comforting and Travis gaining strength and composure from his father.

"Do you remember my friend, Harold Gos-Coyote?" Hank finally asked when he was certain the boy was listening.

"Was he the Indian policeman who died a couple of years ago?"

"That's right. Southern Cheyenne. Trav, before he died we were talking and he told me an ancient legend of his people. I thought it was pretty interesting. Do you want to hear it?"

Travis, his shoulders still shaking, nodded, and Hank continued. "Long ago a man whom the Indians call the Pale God visited among them and taught them how to live."

"A pale god?"

"That's right. A being of pale features whom the Indians revered and worshiped. He performed a lot of miracles, too."

"Was it Jesus?"

"Well, lots of people think it was. But the Indians themselves don't remember who he was anymore. They remember only some of his teachings, and Harold told me one of them.

"According to the legend, this Pale God taught the people that competition was the ugly sister of opposition. It was a counterfeit way of producing strength which was introduced and promoted by the evil one so that people would be destroyed. Do you understand me?"

"Uh, I don't think so," Travis responded.

"Okay, let me say it this way. The Creator, or

God, allowed us to have opposition so we would gain strength by overcoming. Opposition produces strength. The better or the stronger the opposition, the better and stronger we become by facing it.

"Competition, on the other hand, causes us to want to be better than someone else, which in all honesty we can't be. Did God create some of his children to be better than others?"

Travis shook his head.

"You're right, he didn't, at least in a moral sense."

"But, Dad, lots of people think they're better than others."

"Do you think that's a proper attitude, Trav?"

Quickly the boy shook his head again.

"Why not?" Hank asked.

"I don't know. It just doesn't seem right. But I'll tell you, lots of people *are* better than others. Look at Jason and Steve and that creep Alec. They're better than me any day!"

"Yes, they are, at climbing the rope and maybe even other things. But, Trav, does that make them better people?"

"I guess not," the boy determined thoughtfully.

"Of course it doesn't. Everybody's better at something or other, because every person is so different from every other person. And, son, that is how God intended it to be. In fact, I've often said that God's greatest act of creativity is man's individuality. And that, my boy, is the reason why competition is so unfair. How can two or more people, all with different abilities, attitudes, backgrounds, and so on, compete on the same level?"

"They can't, I guess. But I still don't see the

difference between competition and . . . and whatever it was you said."

"Opposition. And to tell you the truth, I'm not sure I know all the differences. However, I *think* it's all attitude, Trav. If someone is our opposition, we want to be as good or as strong as they are. The better they get, the better we need to be to keep up with them. So naturally we want them to get better just as much as we want ourselves to get better.

"On the other hand, if someone is our competition, we want to beat them, to make them lose to us. We want them to become worse than us. When we do that, they feel like you feel today. Do you like that feeling?"

Again Travis shook his head.

"In a nutshell, son, competition demands winners and losers; opposition expects only winners. Which do you think the Lord would approve of?"

"Opposition, I guess."

"Right! All I'm saying, son, is that you are *not* weird because you don't like to lose. God doesn't want any of us to be losers. Besides that, he wants us to be happy when other people *succeed*, not when they fail. That's called charity. How can we have charity if we're hoping they lose so we can win? You see, that's part of the evil that competition does to us.

"Now, forget Coach Gruninger, forget those guys on the ball team, forget those pinewood derbies in Cub Scouts, forget all that. Scores and scoreboards are for coaches and fans, not you. *You* are for you. The only guy on this earth you have to compete with, the only guy you *ever* have to be better than, is Travis Tilby! Understand?"

"I guess so," Travis replied slowly.

"Good. And we'll talk more about this, too, because I think it's pretty important. But meanwhile, come on. Mom's got some watermelon just waiting for us, and believe you me, after weeding that garden we've earned it."

And so together the two walked back to the family, both smiling, both making some resolutions about the future, and neither knowing at all of the glad tidings which were rapidly approaching in the back of old Mr. Larson's new pickup.

Chapter 3
Mr. Larson's Goose

"Fried fish eyes," Mr. Larson croaked feebly as he dragged himself at last out of his finally-stopped truck. "Worst year I ever saw. Nineteen bummers! Imagine that, Hank. Nineteen poor dogged bummer lambs. Why, either those dirty communists are polluting the water, or else Uncle Sam's doing more a-tomic testing down Nevada way. Nineteen bummers. You ever see the like?"

Hank Tilby stood by the tailgate of the pickup with his two oldest sons, shaking his head back and forth. He actually hadn't seen the like, but then he wasn't paying much attention to his landlord's perambulations, either. His attention was on the orphaned lambs, all nineteen of them, and frankly, he was feeling guilty for feeling so good. Those bummer lambs were a financial blessing of the first order for his family, and though he felt bad for old Mr. Larson, he was still grateful for the lambs.

"It's purely awful," Mr. Larson said, spitting into the dirt at his feet. "Is that you, Jase? And Steve? Arid land-o'-Goshen, Hank, but these boys of yours are growing up. Jase here's near as tall as me."

Jason's face showed his surprise, for he was clearly six inches taller than the old man. Hank Tilby grinned and winked at his oldest son, and then turned back to his landlord.

"It's a shame about those ewes and lambs, Mr. Larson. It really is. Still, Lois and the kids and I can pull most of these lambs through. You'll at least have them."

"Don't I know it," the old man growled. "Best lamb raisers in the county, way I see it. By the by, where's that pretty little wife of yours? And little Jenni, too? I thought I saw 'em when I turned in the driveway."

Hank chuckled. "All I can tell you is that they turned tail and ran when they saw you coming. Lois said something about overalls and hair, and Jenni is trying to be like her mom. You know women."

Mr. Larson grinned. "Yep, I know a little about 'em, I guess. Not much more'n that, though. I always figured the best way to understand women was with my hat. Against their logic I usually just grab it and run. Har-har.

"Well, what about it? You and the boys ready to guarantee me the same success you did last year?"

"I don't know about that," Hank replied, "but we'll do our best. Will it be the same deal as last year, Mr. Larson? A mutton and a month's free rent for raising them?"

"Harummmph." The old man coughed as he shuffled his feet in the dirt. "This is getting hard as Manti City water. Can't do the same deal this year, Hank. Somehow it doesn't seem right."

Hank Tilby's face showed his surprise, and for a moment he just stared at the old man.

"Well," he finally said, clearing his throat as he searched for the right words, "I think I understand. Times are tough for everyone, and . . ."

"Arid land-o'-Goshen, Hank," the old man growled. "Let a man finish, will you? I never said you weren't getting a month's rent off, nor a mutton, either. Far as I'm concerned, you still are. What I was trying to say before I was so rudely interrupted was that with these here boys of yours getting bigger right along, it doesn't seem to me like one mutton'd go very far toward feeding them. I was sort of thinking you'd ought to take maybe three this year. Or even better, four. What do you say?"

"I . . . uh . . ."

"Good. I thought you'd see it my way. Four it is! And it ain't charity, either, 'cause you'll earn every blasted one of 'em before the summer's out. Now, where's that youngest boy of yours? Travis, I mean. Where's he at?"

"Trav," Hank called out, his voice thick with sudden emotion because of the generosity of his landlord. "Trav, where are you?"

Slowly the boy shuffled out from behind the tree and stopped.

"Here," he replied slowly.

29

"For Pete's sake," the old man grumbled to himself, "that boy ain't growed an inch in five years. He's still only knee high to a short stump. Come here, son. You and I have got some dealing to do."

Without looking up, Travis shuffled over to the truck and stopped. Jason and Steve, finished with their unloading and penning of the nineteen lambs, stood a little back, wondering just what was going on, and pretty close to finding out.

"Travis," the old man began, "I was down in the meadow west of Chester today, picking up these lambs, when I came onto a poor unfortunate critter that kind of reminded me of Thanksgiving dinner. I scooped him up and was wondering what kind of a rattle-brained fool I was for doing it when I thought of you and that runt lamb you pulled through two summers back.

"Well, what do you know? I asked myself. You know how much you and the wife enjoy roast goose at Thanksgiving, and now you've got an honest-to-goodness wild one and a boy who can coax it into living. Join them up, hand the boy a crisp twenty-dollar bill for his labors, in advance, that is, step back, and all you need to do is watch the feathers grow and wait for November."

"Scrud," Steve grumbled, not quite to himself. "How come Travis gets all the good deals? It ain't . . . isn't fair."

"Steve," Hank warned.

"Well, it isn't. I did as much feeding of that runt lamb as Travis did. Besides, I'm older and . . ."

"Land sakes, boy," Mr. Larson growled. "You sound jealous as sin."

"I ain't jealous! It's just not fair!"

"Steve," Hank tried again, but Mr. Larson cut him off.

"Son," the old man said, putting his arm on the boy's shoulder. "I've come to the conclusion that fair's only fair in the mind of him who calls it, unless it happens to be God. He's fair. The rest of us just do our best to stay close. Now, in my mind you're a big strapping kid that's going to haul a lot of hay for me later on this summer, and earn a fair bundle of pocket change in the process. Trav here can't haul hay because he ain't nowhere near big enough. That's why I give the job to Trav. It's my version of fairness. Understand?"

Steve nodded sullenly, and so the old man turned back to Travis.

"Now, Trav, the little feller's in that box up on top of the oil barrel. Jump up there, take a look, and tell me what you think."

Travis looked from his father to Mr. Larson, acknowledged the man's nod of encouragement with a slight smile, and climbed quickly up into the truck. Carefully he lifted the smashed box off the barrel and placed it down on the bed of the truck. Then, just as cautiously, he pulled back the cardboard flaps, reached in, yelped, and quickly withdrew his hand.

Slowly then a big grin spread across Travis's face, and it was sort of like someone had just turned on the lights. He suddenly came back to life. As he stood there doing his best to ignore Mr. Larson's cackle of glee, his brothers and father became aware for the first time of the sound that would in the coming months drive them all into fits of . . . but there I go again, skipping ahead in my story.

The sound they heard was a hissing sound, somewhat like a snake makes, or maybe like a tire makes when it's going flat, and that's all I'm going to say about it, at least for now.

But, looking happier than a young billy goat in a patch of fresh tin cans, Travis reached back down into that box, grabbed hold of whatever it was that was in there, and pulled it out.

At first about all that anybody could see was a wriggling mass of blackish yellow fuzzy down, which was hissing and stabbing with its bill at anything within reach. But then Trav held it up so he could look into its eyes, hissed back at it in a gentle sort of way, grinned, and nodded with satisfaction when the little creature gradually grew still. Then, with the little gosling, for that is what it was, tucked snugly into the crook of his arm, apparently convinced that it had found its own long-lost mother, Travis climbed carefully down out of the truck.

"Well, arid land-o'-Goshen," old Mr. Larson growled. "How in thunder did you do that?"

"Talked to him," Travis said shyly.

"Go on. You didn't do nothing but hiss. I seen it. You didn't say nothing, and you ain't—"

"Yes, he did," Jason said quickly, interrupting the old man. "I've seen him do it lots of times. Trav can talk to anything, once he hears it talk first. Isn't that right, Trav."

Travis, embarrassed, nodded his head.

"But I don't understand . . ." Mr. Larson began, when Hank Tilby interrupted him.

"Don't even try, Mr. Larson," he said, grinning. "Trav couldn't explain it if he wanted to. But it works. I've seen it, too."

"Hank, that just ain't good enough. That dogged little fiend like to whittled my finger off when I caught him, and now in no time flat that boy of yours has him gentled down like a blooming kitten. Son, I'm busting to know how you did it. Now, go on and tell me."

The boy looked again at his father, almost pleadingly, saw the encouraging nod, took a deep breath, and reluctantly began. "I don't know for sure how it works," he answered quietly. "I just sort of listen to it, think about the sounds it makes, and then I try and copy the sounds."

"That's all?"

"Uh . . . yeah, I guess so."

"It is *not*," Steve mumbled. "There's more! At least *he* says there is."

"Is there?" Mr. Larson asked kindly.

Travis shot a dirty look at his older brother, knew that he could do no more to get even with him at the moment, sighed, and finally spoke.

"Well," he continued slowly, "maybe a little."

"Tell me, son. I'd like to hear."

"No, you wouldn't," Travis replied with sudden determination. "Nobody believes me, and everybody laughs when I try to explain!"

"Laughs? I wouldn't laugh, son. I've seen it, and I want to know. Do you talk out loud to these animals, or what?"

Again the boy sighed. Overhead a small puffball of a cloud drifted across the sun, and he watched as its shadow slipped down the field, covered the old barn, and began to climb the side of the mountain beyond. How he would have loved to be there with it, alone on the mountain, lying back in a fragrant sagebrush just watching the clouds and dreaming. That was the part of Sanpete Valley that he loved best, the quiet and the mountain. It was always close, and—

"Travis?"

Startled, Travis realized that he had been dreaming again, a habit which all too frequently got him into trouble.

"No," he answered quickly, "not really. I hardly ever talk out loud when I'm telling it something. Not at first, at least. I sort of think to it, kind of like I'm its mother or something. Like I said to Chester here, that—"

"Who?" the old man asked, surprised.

"Chester. That's the goose's name, you know."

"Course I didn't know. Who named it?"

"You did, I guess," Travis replied quickly. "Or maybe I did. Anyway, you said you caught him near Chester, so that's his name."

"Makes sense, I suppose. Go on. You sort of think to it, you say?"

"Yeah, sort of. When I'm making its noises, I think to it like I'm talking to it or something. I told Chester not to worry because I was going to help him and be his family. You know, that kind of stuff."

"And you think he heard . . . I mean understood you?"

"I don't know," Travis replied frankly. "I heard him, though. Just not with my ears. He was fighting because he was scared and lonely. That's why I told him what I did. What do they eat?"

Amazed, Mr. Larson shook his head and ignored the boy's question. "Incredible," he breathed. "I never heard the like. You talk to sheep, too?"

"And cows," Jason added quickly before his younger brother could respond, "and calves, and the dog, and some coyotes once. He even talks to the pigs, but they're so dumb that they don't even listen."

"Not dumb," Travis said defensively, "just selfish. They only like to listen to themselves. I don't like pigs very much. I . . . hey, this little goose is missing a foot! What happened to it?"

"I don't know, son. He was that way when I found him. There'd been a fire there, though, and someone had done a lot of shooting. Three or four geese were dead, and when I was putting out the last of the fire, I found this little critter kicking around in the ashes. The way I see it, he might have lost his foot in that fire. Or else maybe the shooting. I don't know.

"Whichever, losing a foot didn't slow him down much. He can hop faster than I can run. I near killed myself trying to catch him, but I kept after him because I knew he'd die if I didn't get him, and I couldn't see much sense in having him die uselessly."

"Why would he have died?"

35

"Don't nobody know nothing around here but me? He'd die 'cause he'll never fly. A goose without both feet can't fly, you know, so he's sort of lost the race before he even got entered. Why, I never saw such a . . ."

And that was when Mr. Larson saw the tears start up in Travis's eyes. The boy turned quickly away, and the old man was still wondering what he should say when Travis turned back, doing his best to smile, and held the little goose out before him.

"Go on, Chester," he urged gently. "Tell Mr. Larson thank you for saving your life. Tell him that your missing leg won't matter none. Tell him you ain't a loser, nohow. You and me, we'll just figure out some other way for you to get along. Go on, now, tell him."

Then, while the gosling squirmed frantically, Trav made small hissing sounds to it. And suddenly, while everyone watched, Chester turned his small bright eyes upon the old man, bobbed his head up and down a few times, and then squirmed to get back against Travis's chest.

Well, frankly, old Mr. Larson was stunned. He looked to Hank Tilby for support, but got only shrugged shoulders and a proud smile for a response. Jason and Steve were grinning as well, and when he turned finally to Travis for some sort of help, the boy was already walking away. And while he walked, his tears and his thirteen-year-old clouds of depression were lifting already from his heart, being replaced by a happy smile of anticipation. He was on his way to introduce Chester

36

to his mother and little sister, he was on his way to teach a baby goose to fly, and he was excited!

So, in spite of its unlikely appearance, that little baby Canadian honker Chester-goose, with its fuzzy body, its beady little eyes, and its one lonely leg, had already started to work its miracle. And like I said, that's what this story is about. Miracles.

Chapter 4
Jenni Declares Faith

Once in the house, Travis looked for his mom, couldn't find her, and so went to Jenni's room. There he found his seven-year-old sister playing schoolteacher in front of the mirror, a game which, with minor variations, she played almost constantly. Gently he pulled the tiny goose from his shirt so that Jenni could see it, and only then did he interrupt her very animated lesson.

"This is Chester, Jen. Mr. Larson's hired me to raise him. Ain't he a beaut?"

"Isn't, Trav," the little girl corrected instantly.

"Yeah, isn't he?"

"That's *much* better. Gee. Can I touch him?"

"Sure. You can even hold him if you're careful. Here. Use both hands, now."

Carefully Jenni took the goose from Travis and held it against her chest. "Oh, Trav, he's so soft. And warm, too. He's the most cuddliest thing I ever saw. But he's shaking, and his heart's going real fast. How come?"

"He's scared, Jen. I guess he thinks we're going to hurt him again."

"Again? But what's ... Oh, Trav, look at his foot. His leg is gone! Oh, poor little thing. What happened to it?"

"I don't know. Mr. Larson found him that way. Maybe he lost it in a fire or something."

"Does it hurt?"

"I don't think so. I think it's been gone a long time, maybe even since he was bor—er—I mean hatched. But look at this. Mr. Larson gave me this twenty dollars to raise him."

"Can I help?" Jenni asked as she cradled the gosling close to her chest.

"Sure. Geese like girls about as much as they do boys, I guess. There ain't no—"

"Trav, it's *isn't*! You know what Mommy says about that word."

"Yeah, I forgot. Anyway, there isn't no reason why he can't be your pet, too."

Jenni giggled as she cuddled the tiny goose, for she loved the softness of its down pressed gently against her cheek.

"How about Steve and Jason?" she suddenly asked.

"Huh?"

"Can they help grow Chester, too?"

"Uh-huh, if they want. Jason's already told me that he'll help build a pen when Chester gets bigger. I'll bet Steve'll want to help, too. Chester ain't ... isn't mine, you know. He's all of us's."

"What if Chester doesn't like those guys?"

"Oh, he will."

"But what if he doesn't? That one lamb you raised sure didn't."

"Jen, you're just like growed-up women, always arguing a man, always asking tomfool questions that there ain't—"

"Isn't," the little girl corrected, sounding exasperated.

"All right, that there isn't no answers to."

"That's better, Trav. I like it when you talk right."

"Yeah, me, too, I guess. Now, come on. Let's go figure out where Chester's going to sleep."

Going quickly to the boys' bedroom, Travis handed Chester once again to Jenni, pulled the old toy box from the closet, dumped the broken-down toys from it, wadded up a pillowcase, placed it into one corner, and gently laid Chester upon it. He stood up, grinning.

For a moment the gosling held still, but then with a hiss it hopped up onto its one foot and slammed its body into the side of the large wooden box. Down it went, but was instantly up again, slamming itself against the side once more, intent upon escape.

"Trav," Jenni screamed, "he's going to get hurt!"

"No, he ain't," Travis reassured her. "When he hurts bad enough, he'll stop. That's how Dad says critters learn."

"But he'll get away."

"He can't do that, either, Jen. He needs two legs to jump that high, and he can't do it without . . ."

And then Travis realized, finally, the full implication of the tiny goose having only one foot. Filled with sudden compassion, he reached into the box, took Chester out, and began hissing gently. Gradually the little goose began to calm, and only after it was snuggled against him did he speak.

"Jen," he whispered as he blinked back two large eyefuls of tears, "Chester won't ever be able to fly."

"Why not, Trav? He's got wings, hasn't he?"

"Yeah, but for some birds it takes more than that. Mr. Larson said that geese can't fly with only one foot, and last year in school I read why. I just now remembered it."

"Well? How come?"

"It's 'cause they need a running start."

"Really?"

"Yeah. And Chester can't run. He can only hop, and that can't get him going fast enough."

"Gee, Trav, you're sure smart."

Travis looked down at his sister, his heart still filled with sorrow for the little bird in his arms. "Yeah, I guess maybe I am, in some ways. But I've always wanted to fly, and I've never figured out how. That ain't too smart. Now I've got to forget me and figure out how to get Chester here to fly. I don't know if I can."

"Oh," Jenni replied, her voice filled with pride, "you'll think of something. You always do. You're an inventory."

Travis looked again at his little sister, a large grin spreading across his face. "That's an *inventor*, Jen, not an inventory."

"Oh," she giggled. Then, pointing a finger at her

hand, she rolled her eyes and spoke again, her voice slow and dramatic. "I must be going cuckoo in the head, I think. I could have *sworn* you were an inventory."

Now Travis rolled his eyes. "Jen, do you always have to be an actress?"

Jenni giggled once more, her giggle sounding more like the cackling of a chicken than anything else. Travis grinned and waited patiently until she stopped, for he knew that she would only laugh harder if he tried to stop her.

"Well," he said when she was finally out of breath, "inventor or not, I've got to hurry. Mr. Larson only gave Chester to me until Thanksgiving. Then he and Mrs. Larson are going to eat him for dinner."

"Oh, no!" Jenni gasped, her face suddenly serious.

"Well, that's what he said. But somehow I'm going to teach Chester to fly, so he can get away. They *can't* eat Chester."

"I know what we can do, Trav. We can pray! God won't let Chester get eaten up. He *loves* him. Just like Mommy says he loves us. If we all be good and pray, then Jesus will save Chester. I'll betcha he will!"

"I don't know, Jen. It seems kind of funny praying for a goose."

"Why? Didn't God make gooses?"

"It's geese, and yes he did, but . . ."

"Then it isn't funny. My Sunday school teacher says for us to pray about everything. Chester's part of everything, isn't he?"

"Yeah, but . . ."

"So there! We *can* pray about him!"

"Jenni's right, Travis."

Both children spun around, and both were surprised to see their mother standing in the doorway, a slight smile on her lips.

"If you pray about Chester and have faith," she continued, "it will work out for the best. The Good Lord always answers sincere prayers. But I want you to remember that the goose *does* belong to Mr. Larson, and he has the right to do with it what he wants."

"He was God's goose first," Jenni replied quickly.

Lois looked at her little daughter, amazed as always by the deep wisdom the little girl so frequently displayed. What happened, she wondered, that children's faith became so muddled by the time they were in their teens? It was a sad thing, but it was certainly true.

"Yes, Jenni," she finally replied. "Chester is God's little goose, but he is also Mr. Larson's. It's like you are God's little girl, but you are also mine. Do you understand?"

Jenni nodded, and so Lois went on. "Besides, Trav has taken Mr. Larson's money to raise this creature, which means that he has agreed to do it. Isn't that so, Trav?"

Now Travis nodded, and though he wouldn't raise his eyes, Lois sensed his desire and determination. Knowing that further talk about her son learning to face responsibility would accomplish nothing, at least at the moment, she wisely changed the subject.

"Now, let me see this little orphan of yours," she

said eagerly, pushing aside the feelings of dread which were already beginning to rumble about in her heart.

Travis looked up, saw that she was smiling, and so, proudly, he showed his mother the baby gosling. And I have to tell you that Lois Tilby oohed and aahed and was just as sincerely motherly over that dirty little goose as Jenni had been. I'd also better tell you that she noticed right off how Travis had wadded up a good pillowcase and dumped it in the bottom of the toy box. And, much to her natural dismay, she also saw the brownish spot right in the middle of that same pillowcase. Still, that good woman said nothing. She just did her best to smile, for it was always in her mind, even on hard days, that she was raising and protecting children, not pillowcases and other such noneternal stuff.

"Well," she said finally as she handed the fuzzy creature back to her son, "don't you think it's time we fed this little baby of yours?"

Travis and Jenni both nodded and followed their mother down into the kitchen. Then, while Travis held the little gosling and hissed thoughts of comfort to it, his mother squirted drops of diluted Cream of Wheat cereal down its throat with an eyedropper.

At first Chester resisted, but Travis kept hissing and stroking and his mother kept squirting until finally the little goose realized that it was getting food. From then on it was like pouring water down a gopher hole. There was just no bottom.

That little bird ate more Cream of Wheat than Travis ever had.

Satiated at last, however, the gosling pushed its head up under Travis's arm, wriggled a little, and found comfort there. Then, with a last twist, it turned its head, fixed its bright black eyes on Jenni and then Lois, bobbed its head up and down a few times, ducked under Travis's arm again, and was still.

Lois and Jenni both giggled, Travis grinned, and then quietly he crept back up the stairs while his mother and sister followed. There he placed Chester on the pillowcase, covered him with part of it, and sat back and sighed.

"Gee, Mom," he whispered happily, "ain't he something?"

Lois looked down at her son, put her hand gently on his head, mussed his hair, blinked back a couple of tears, and spoke. "He certainly is, Trav. He's almost as 'something' as you are. I'm glad you found each other. Now, come on. Sitting here dreaming surely *ain't* getting your chores done."

Jenni gasped, Travis looked up at his mother in shock, suddenly realized that she was teasing him and reminding him all at once, and then with an embarrassed grin, Travis led his mother and sister from the bedroom, leaving Chester alone to dream the sweet dreams of freedom enjoyed, as you most likely already know, by all baby geese, wild or otherwise.

Chapter 5
Talking in the Morning

Have you ever lain awake, early in the morning, and heard the murmur of voices coming from your parents' bedroom? There's something very curious about that sound, for though it is neither distinct nor revealing, it is nevertheless one of the most reassuring sounds that a child can ever hear.

Now, I'm not even going to pretend to tell you why that's so, for I don't know. I suspect, though, that it has to do with caring, or love. Any child knows, somehow, that when parents talk in the morning, they are discussing their children, deciding how to help them become better and therefore more happy kids. The understanding that their parents love them enough to discuss them, and the soft murmuring sound that carries such understanding, will give any child a sense of security.

Of course most parents don't realize the good they are doing, but they talk early in the morning, anyway, for any number of reasons, and so it all works out fine. Hank and Lois Tilby were that way.

They talked almost every morning, about every imaginable subject, and they were innocently unaware that they were blessing their children's lives with the love-filled sound of their quiet voices. But they were, and it's one of those predawn conferences that I'd like to tell you about.

It wasn't yet light that particular morning, but Hank had been lying awake for some time, thinking about what his youngest son had told him the day before. An early morning breeze was fluttering the curtains at the window, chilling the room, and he was considering getting up and closing the sash when his wife spoke.

"Don't close it," she said sleepily, somehow reading his mind. "It's cold now, but later we'll be glad for the coolness."

Surprised, Hank turned and looked over at his wife. In the darkness her features were indistinct, but her dark hair was fluffed out in silhouette against the whiteness of the pillow, and in his mind he could see her face clearly. Mentally he traced the squareness of her forehead, the thin line of her eyebrows, the dainty sharpness of her nose, the generous fullness of her lips and determined tilt of her chin. He thought, too, of the gentle compassion that filled her soft brown eyes, and he knew that of all her features, that gentleness was the one he treasured most.

How he loved her, and how he appreciated the

fact that her beauty, as radiant and visible as it was, came more from within than from without. What would he do, he wondered, if one day she was not at his side, loving and supporting him? How on earth could he ever live without her?

As the familiar aching emptiness filled his chest, as it did each time he thought of the possibility of losing either Lois or one of the children, Hank closed his eyes and his mind against the painful swelling of emotion. He knew he would survive such a loss, should it ever occur, for his faith in the eternal nature of his family was strong. Yet his love for his wife and children made thoughts of such a possibility so painful that he hated having them, and he fought them back each time he did.

"How do you do that?" he finally asked, mentally succeeding in changing the subject.

"What?"

"How did you know what I was thinking?"

Lois giggled. "I don't know, honey. I know we think a lot alike, and closing the window is what I was thinking of doing. When you stiffened to move, I just guessed. That's all."

For a moment there was silence, and in the stillness Hank rolled over and stared upward.

"Are you worried about Travis?" Lois suddenly asked.

Hank chuckled. "See, there you go again. Whatever happened to privacy around here? I can't even have privacy in my mind anymore."

Quickly Lois reached over and took her husband's hand. "I'm sorry," she whispered. "I don't mean to pry."

"You're not prying, honey. I just don't know what to do. Travis is hurting, and I'm as much the cause of his pain as anyone."

"Hank . . ."

"It's true, Lois. Do you know what he told me? He thinks he's a loser. He thinks he's a loser because he never wins at anything, including all the little contests I set up here at home. He says he hates school, church, and even home sometimes, because he's a loser everywhere."

"But he doesn't mean that, Hank. He doesn't understand . . ."

"Yes, he does, Lois, and that's what scares me. He understands perfectly. Do you know, lying here this morning I've thought about it, and almost everything Travis is involved in is based on the principle of competition. It's hardly different for kids than it is for adults."

"But what's so bad about that?" Lois questioned. "Boys love competition."

"Yes," Hank replied, "they do. Or at least most do. I always did, and Jason and Steve seem to. But yesterday out in the orchard I met a boy who doesn't. Isn't that sad, that I don't really meet my own son until he's thirteen? And it's just as sad that I don't know he's dying inside because he sees himself as a loser."

"Hank, you're being too harsh on yourself."

"Am I? I made a contest yesterday of weeding the garden. Who lost? Travis. Could he do anything about it? Not likely. He's the smallest, and can't work as hard or as fast as the other boys. Last Sunday we made a contest out of finding

49

Scriptures in the Bible. Travis lost. Why? Because he doesn't know them as well as the other boys. I teased him about losing, and I know that made him feel worse than ever. Am I being too harsh on myself?"

"But not all his contests are with older boys, Hank. And you don't set all of them up, either."

"That's true, but they *are* all contests, all programs designed with competition in mind. And Lois, contests between people mean that we create losers even more than winners, and in much greater numbers. Harold Gos-Coyote told me that once, but it didn't register. I never understood what Harold was saying until I saw the pain in my own son.

"Take the pinewood derby in Cub Scouts, for example. Thirty-two boys raced their cars last year, six or seven won something, and twenty-five boys went home feeling like losers. Three years Travis raced cars, remember, and all three years he lost. Was it his fault? Hardly. It was probably mine, because I didn't have the several hours to give him that the project should have taken."

"Well, you did get it built."

"Sure I did, in a three-hour crash program that was a poor substitute for what I should have done. Yet it was Travis who lost, not me. What does that do to his self-esteem? And what kind of a program is that for a church which teaches a gospel of love, beginning with love for self?"

"I'd never thought of it like that before," Lois said quietly.

"Neither had I, honey, not until yesterday when

Travis gave me a glimpse of the pain in his soul, pain caused by what Harold once called the evil of competition. The sad thing, Lois, is that this happens everywhere, not just with Travis.

"Our church has ball tournaments where winning frequently becomes so important that boys and girls, and even men and women who ought to be exercising love for each other, spend their time instead fighting and yelling and filling themselves with bitterness and animosity. A few excel in these activities, most fail, and a very few conscientious souls who understand that the true point of church activity is bringing about the love of Christ among people resist such policies.

"But Lois, it's pretty hard to be a discriminate resister. If you rebel against one thing, then you're considered a rebel against all things. If a person rebels against competition, especially when it's so socially accepted, then that person is branded as evil or strange or weird. Then, even though that individual is right, he or she loses, anyway. They lose in all directions. That's what has happened to Travis."

Lois sat up and gazed into her husband's eyes. "You really feel strongly about this, don't you?"

Suddenly Hank grinned sheepishly. "I don't know," he replied slowly. "I do, and yet I don't know if I do. It's all so new to me. I love sports, and you know what a fierce competitor I've always been. It's just that Travis has shown me another side of things. He showed me that not all people enjoy the same things I do, and the pain he suffers when he is forced to participate in them is causing me to reevaluate. My mind feels like it is going in circles, and I don't know where it will end up. I will say, though, that the more I think about the principle of competition, the more problems I see with it."

"Okay, if competition is a problem, then what's the solution?"

Hank gazed at his wife, amazed as always by the practical side of her nature. She had a way of getting down to the nitty-gritty of things that was very beneficial, though at times her directness was disconcerting.

"Sweetheart," he sighed as he squeezed Lois's hand, "that's the stickler. I honestly don't know. Harold said it was in accepting opposition rather than competition, and I suspect he's right, though I don't yet understand fully what he meant."

"Could it mean attitude changes more than anything else?"

"Probably, at least to begin with. But whatever, there *is* an answer, I'm sure of it. And for Travis's sake I'm going to find it. I can't let that boy grow up thinking he's a loser just because he enjoys different types of activities than I do."

"And . . . and Travis really does feel that he's a loser?" Lois asked, her voice filled with pain.

"That's right. He's so down on himself because everyone else seems to be that he doesn't blame Coach Gruninger at all for what was done to him on Field Day. Trav sincerely thinks it's himself that's weird. He's convinced that he'll always be a loser, and will never become a man because of it."

Lois was silent for a moment, thinking, feeling,

hurting. "I should have known," she replied at last. "I should have recognized it."

"I should have, too, but I didn't."

"But, Hank, I've studied it a little, and there are symptoms I should have seen. When a person has a high level of self-esteem, he is happy. He has confidence in his abilities, his achievement level is high, he is open and friendly toward other people, and so on. I've just described the old Travis, the one we've lived with and enjoyed for the past twelve years.

"Low self-esteem creates the opposite effect, and it's easy to see that that's what has happened with Trav. He's withdrawn from us, he doesn't try very hard to do anything, he doesn't say much, the least little thing hurts his feelings, he cries easily, and I could go on and on. Oh, why haven't I been able to see that?"

"Where did you learn all that?"

"In school. From Drs. Burr and Barlow. Why?"

"I'm . . . I'm just impressed," Hank answered honestly. "I should have noticed it, too, and yet I didn't."

"But you had no training . . ."

"No, but the Bible says the same thing, and I *have* studied *it*. In Proverbs the Lord says that as a man thinketh in his heart, so is he. That's just what you're saying. A man becomes what he thinks he is. It also says in the New Testament that a man should love his neighbor as himself. If you don't like yourself, you fulfill that commandment by not liking others. It's actually very clear."

"Yes," Lois responded thoughtfully, "I guess it

53

is. But what . . . how do we help Trav overcome this?"

Hank turned and looked at his wife. "You know the answer to that," he chided gently. "You do it all the time."

"What?"

"Service, Lois. Losing yourself in another's life helps you find yourself."

For a long moment Lois stared at the ceiling. "You know," she said, "I remember a study where students were asked to spend one week building another individual's self-esteem. They did, and it worked, but the unexpected side effect was that the students' own self-esteem grew even more. And . . . and *that's* what you did with Jason and Steve, isn't it, when you asked them to watch out for Trav?"

Hank grinned and remained silent.

"It's working, too," Lois stated thoughtfully, "especially with Jason."

"It'll work with Steve as well," Hank declared. "It may take a little longer, but it'll work. So far, though, it hasn't helped Travis very much, and he's the one I'm really worried about."

"Who can we have Travis help?"

"I don't know. That's what has me stumped. He already loves Jenni and does all he can for her. I'd tell him to work on his big brothers, but I know right now they wouldn't let him, at least enough to do any good. Beyond them, I don't know where to turn."

"Oh, Hank," Lois cried softly, her voice choking with emotion, "what are we going to do?"

Outside, the sky had grown light, a rooster off toward town was crowing with the excitement of the new day, and suddenly the alarm went off.

Hank reached over, poked it with his finger, and then rolled his feet out onto the floor. "Well," he said slowly, "I don't know what you're going to do, but I'm going to get up. If the boys and I don't get started mighty soon on the chores, we'll be late for church."

"Hank . . ." Lois pleaded.

Plopping backward once more onto the bed, Hank rolled over and gazed into his wife's lovely and love-filled eyes. "Honey," he said gently as he caressed her cheek, "I honestly don't know what to do. But I think if we exercise our faith it will work out. Somehow the Lord will help us find a way to convince that boy that he's capable of great things. We know he is. We just need to help him believe it. Now, give me a Sunday morning kiss. Maybe that'll give me the strength to go face old Gerty and her corral full of smelly unmentionable you-know-what."

Lois giggled, the kiss was given, morning prayer was offered, and both left the bedroom with an increased awareness of the suffering of a little boy who had been loaned to them, by God, as their son. They also left with a determination to find some way of helping him to know how great he really was.

Chapter 6
The Rope

Now, because this story is sort of two or three stories all mixed in together, I've got to step back again and bring you up to date. But don't worry. This'll only happen this one last time, and then we can just sort of sail forward together. Agreed?

The Larson place that the Tilbys rented wasn't much of a farm as far as farms went, for it was only about five acres, and most of that was in pasture and rocks and sage. In other words, not much grew on it. However, it was still a great farm, for it was a wonderful place to raise a flock of kids, the main and only crop that Hank and Lois Tilby were interested in raising.

And why was it such a good place for that? you ask. Well, because there was space there. Lots of it! And for some reason that I can't begin to explain, kids seem to thrive on open air and space. There were also chores to do, and I do mean chores.

Plenty of them. Those chores made the kids grumble at times, but they also taught them how to work, an experience which their mother said they all greatly needed. So there you have the two best reasons why the Tilbys rented old Mr. Larson's farm. Space and work, both of which resulted in a whole lot of family togetherness.

Of course there was also the economy, which made it impossible for Hank to buy a place of his own. But there's no point in talking about that, so I won't. Except I guess I should say how Hank and Lois were doing the very best they could to hold things together, what with times so tough, and they were mostly doing a fine job of it, too, with all the kids pitching in and doing their share.

But I don't want to give you the wrong impression here, either. Sure the kids milked the cow and cared for the other animals and spent a whole lot of time gardening and irrigating and harvesting and painting and fixing up around the place, which most anyone who knows anything at all about anything would call work. But that wasn't all they did, not by a long shot. Mainly, in spite of everything else, those Tilby kids had fun.

Both Jason and Steve were Eagle Scouts, so both of them could borrow the old single-shot .22 from their dad. This they did, as often as they could afford shells, and then, with Travis tagging along, they'd spend endless hours up on the mountain, plinking. And what was funny about that was that Travis was usually the best shot. Why, one time he brought a magpie out of the air at over two hundred yards with that single-shot .22, and I don't know of anyone who can shoot much better than that!

Besides shooting, there were also the horses to ride, and endless games to be played out in the pasture and beyond, especially at night, when games are always the most fun.

And though it's going to sound strange to say it, the greatest treasure on their property, and the source of the most fun to all of them, was the old barn down against the back fence, the one that hadn't been used for a little longer than forever.

Every one of the boys loved that barn, and Jenni liked going there, too, though that was dangerous if her brothers happened to be using it that day as a clubhouse or whatever. The barn had an old manger, a hayloft filled with musty hay, a couple of boxes for pigeons to roost in, a real high loft which was the clubhouse and hiding place for filched crackers, Jell-O, and the like, and a new addition which swung now from the highest beam in the barn.

That addition, of course, was *The Rope*.

Now, that rope cost sixty-one dollars and eighty-seven cents, a tidy fortune when the Tilby family budget had already been stretched beyond breaking. I wasn't going to spend a lot of time telling you about how they raised the money for it, but it's part of the story, so I'll tell you quickly that on Sunday afternoon after church Hank and Lois called an emergency session of the family council, and that's where it happened.

Travis, still upset, was quiet with his pain, doing his best to suffer alone. His brothers, though, were filled with all sorts of crazy talk of revenge against Coach Gruninger and Alec for what they had done, and their attitudes worried Lois so much that she told them so.

"Boys," she stated quietly, "your great-grandfather Hyrum Soderberg used to tell me when I was a little girl that a man wasn't smart playing leapfrog with a unicorn, and that there were better ways of getting the point. I think we can beat Coach Gruninger at his own game, and put Alec to silence. But I think we need to do it in *our* way, not theirs. Hank, how much does a climbing rope cost?"

Well, the upshot of that question was that Travis gave the twenty dollars old Mr. Larson had paid him in advance for raising his goose, less of course his church tithing, Jason and Steve gave ten and five dollars each, Jenni put in thirty-nine cents, Lois and Hank anted up the difference, and The Rope was purchased. Travis was in competition with himself, The Rope was the opposition, the entire family became his cheering section, and strangely enough Chester became head cheerleader.

And could that little goose ever cheer! Every morning from the day they hung that rope, and as soon as the chores were done, Travis and Chester were off to the old barn. Once there, Trav would start climbing and Chester would start fussing about on the ground, flapping and hopping and making more noise than a convention of happy hound dogs. That was how Chester cheered.

To begin with, Jason and Steve went with Travis to the barn as well. But gradually they lost interest, for no matter what they did, no matter how many times they showed Travis how to climb that rope, he couldn't do it. Steve would hold the bottom of the rope, Jason would perch on a bale of hay to give instructions, and Travis would make his attempt. But no matter how high he jumped, no matter how hard he strained, no matter how he twisted his legs around it, he could never even reach the halfway mark on that rope.

"No!" Jason would shout, his voice filled with frustration. "Not that way. Reach!"

And Trav would reach, but it was never far enough.

"Here," Steve would growl, his own frustration evident. "Let me show you how."

And up the rope he would scamper, almost effortlessly, it seemed to Travis, all the time saying, "See, do it this way. Use your hands like I do, and use your feet and legs like this. And count, for crying out loud. It really helps."

And so Travis would stare, open-mouthed, and then, mimicking his brothers in every way, he would do his best to do as they did. "One, two, three . . . four . . ." And that would be all. He could go no higher.

Chester, on the ground, would hop back and forth, hissing and making his clicking noise, cheering and growing more agitated by the moment because of Jason's and Steve's loud voices. But even this would not help, and Travis, exhausted and discouraged, would sink at last into the hay, once again a failure.

Travis failed in other things, too, for he was an

average boy who made plenty of foolish decisions in the process of gaining maturity. One of those decisions, for instance, nearly cost him the support of his mother, for without really thinking about it he used her satin pillowcase, which she had received as a wedding gift from her grandmother, as Chester's bed.

"Travis," Lois shrieked when she saw the condition of the treasured gift, "what on *earth* are you thinking of? Don't you know that my grandmother made that for me? It's ruined now, thanks to that stupid goose, and . . ."

"See," the boy wailed, fighting back the sudden tears which so embarrassed him whenever they bubbled up, "I never do *anything* right! Everything I touch is ruined! Now even Chester's bad, all because of me!"

Turning then, the boy picked up his goose and fled outside, convinced more than ever that he was worse than useless and that he could never do anything right. Nor did it help to know that his mother had every right to be angry. He *should* have known better. Only he hadn't, and more than likely, he never would.

In spite of all this pain and agony, however, there was one ray of light for Travis, and that was his goose. Chester grew daily, and daily he became more fun to be around. At first Travis carried the little gosling, but as the days passed and the goose grew, Travis found that there was no need to carry him at all. In fact, Chester became Travis's shadow, following him everywhere with that strange hop-and-flutter gait which he developed to get along.

61

By the time June was half over, he was nearly two feet tall, his gray down had been replaced by beautiful silken feathers, his wingspan was wider by far than Travis could reach, and he had a personality all his own. In fact, it was obvious to Travis that Chester thought himself a human, and when he was denied certain privileges, like sleeping in his bed with him, Chester acted thoroughly offended.

Chester had only a short stump where his leg had been, but the young goose didn't seem to notice. With his wings extended for balance he hopped about on his foot as though that was the only way geese had ever been designed to travel.

And travel Chester did, up and down the road, all throughout the yard, into the house if a door was left open, and even occasionally into the yards of the neighbors. But again, I don't want to get ahead of myself, so let me just say that Chester simply seemed to love going places.

Chester also loved to play tag, and he enjoyed especially being chased by Travis. Off he'd go with Travis in hot pursuit, hopping along and honking crazily, his long neck extended like an antenna, around and around the yard. That would go on until Chester decided the race had lasted long enough, and then suddenly he would turn and, with wings extended, go after Travis, raising a verbal storm as he did so. At last, when both were tired, Travis would roll to the ground and Chester would hop onto his chest, where he would dart his long neck back and forth, trying to nibble the boy's ears. That was how Chester played with Travis.

With Jenni, however, Chester behaved very differently, for with her he seldom played tag. He simply stood silently beside her, his head resting in her hands, while he gazed with his soft eyes up into her face. If she walked anywhere, the goose hopped along beside her, silently, except for a quiet clicking, staying as close to her as he could. Those two were Chester's only real friends.

Chester tolerated Travis's mother, usually ignoring her unless she came near. Then he would hop away, clicking rapidly in warning. At first this made Lois nervous, but gradually she relaxed and soon reached the point where she talked to the goose almost as easily as Travis and Jenni did. Sometimes when she did this, Hank would tease her, but even so she kept on talking, simply because she enjoyed the unique personality of the goose.

But no one else in the family really enjoyed Chester. As far as Steve and Jason and their father Hank were concerned, Chester was an official pain in the neck. The bird was nothing more than a pest, and their dislike ranged from passive when Chester wasn't around to extremely active when the goose was nearby.

At first the two boys had been intrigued by the unusual pet, and they had held him and tried to care for him just like Travis. But then one night during supper, when they were talking about the goose, Travis asked if his father or his brothers knew why, in a flying formation of geese, one side of the "V" was always longer than the other. No one seemed to know, but Steve was especially in-sistent about learning.

"You really don't know?" Travis asked innocently.

"Come on. How could I? Now, why *is* one side longer than the other?"

"Because it has more geese in it," Travis replied casually.

For an instant there was silence, but then Hank, his glass to his mouth, suddenly coughed and started laughing. Soon everyone but Steve joined in, Chester started honking, and Travis enjoyed his moment of triumph.

Sadly, however, it backfired, for after that Steve turned against Travis and his pet. At first it was only a little, but soon Steve was openly making fun of the goose. That spread from Chester to Travis, and the whole thing quickly got out of hand.

Things got even worse when Alec Suggins started driving past the Tilby home with Sheryl Hanson snuggled up next to him, shouting taunting little remarks as he roared by. Of course Sheryl wasn't really snuggled, she *did* live on the same road as the Tilbys, which left no other way for Alec to have gone, she didn't shout any taunts, Alec's re-marks concerned Travis and the rope rather than Jason, and so on.

Thing was, Jason liked Sheryl so much, though he'd never dared even talk to her, that Alec's activ-ities seemed like an intentional affront to him, not to Travis. In the agony of his wounded pride he concluded without even intending to that Travis and Chester were the cause of the whole painful thing, and so he turned on them as viciously as Steve had done.

Travis, feeling more lonely and less successful than ever, leaned on Chester for companionship and acceptance. He played with the bird, he took him swimming down at Les Simms's pond, he took him hiking with him up on the mountain, and daily, in spite of Mr. Larson's and his parents' words of caution, he invested his heart and grew more and more to love the young goose.

Chester reciprocated in kind, and seemed to come to the conclusion finally that Travis and maybe Jenni, rather than the entire Tilby family, were his flock. Those two he loved as only a goose can love, while the rest of the Tilby family the goose regarded with considerably less esteem.

Time passed, Chester reached adult size, and one morning when Steve approached the goose, he spread his huge wings, lowered his head, and hissing loudly, he charged. Steve, yelping with fear, beat a hasty retreat to the house, where his horror story about the dangerous goose grew in direct proportion to the number of times he told it.

Jason then ventured forth and met with the same fate, except that Chester caught the boy's finger in its beak. Yelling, Jason kicked the goose in an attempt to get free, and from that moment on, each considered the other as public and private enemy number one.

And then, to cap it all, that very evening Travis's father, stepping out of his car, found himself confronted by the same hissing monster, and if it hadn't been for the pleadings of Travis, Jenni, and their mother, Chester could easily have gone back to old Mr. Larson that very night.

He didn't, but the goose had lost three valuable friends, and sadly, Travis's esteem sank lower than ever.

JULY

Chapter 7
Troubles at the Tilbys'

Friend or otherwise, however, no one closely associated with the Tilby family was spared Chester's influence that summer. In one way or another that goose got to everyone and everything around. For instance, one of Chester's favorite objects of persecution was the family cow, whose name was Gertrude, or Gerty, for short.

Gerty, for some reason, was terrified of the goose. Chester quickly realized that and took a fiendish delight in harassing the gentle old cow in every way he could.

For example, whenever Gerty went for a drink, Chester would hop quietly up to the water barrel, doing his best to avoid being seen. Then when Gerty had her nose fairly buried in the cool water, Chester would rise up from behind the barrel like a devil incarnate.

Gerty, totally discombobulated, would stagger

backward in fear and, stumbling over her own feet, wheel and retreat in awkward disgrace to the far end of the pasture. There she would stand in wide-eyed terror, her sides heaving, while Chester hopped back and forth along the outside of the fence, his own chest puffed up with pompous, un-righteous pride.

Well, as you can imagine, Gerty learned quickly. It wasn't too long before she determined to die of thirst rather than face the watering trough and the crazy fowl which seemed to inhabit it. Finally, when her milk started to dry up, the family found themselves taking turns leading her to water, a time-consuming task which none of them relished.

After several days of family members dragging Gerty to water, Travis was given orders by his parents to tie his pet up until a pen could be built for him. Travis, however, fought the idea tooth and nail, tied the goose only occasionally, and then left the knot intentionally loose. Thus, Chester's depre-dations continued.

Other objects of persecution for Chester were the bummer lambs, which followed one another to the far side of the pasture in terror whenever the goose hissed at one of them. Chester also declared war on all dogs, neighborhood cats fled in haste whenever Chester appeared, and twice the crazy bird frightened the two horses so badly that they leaped the fence and cost the family hours in rounding them up.

Besides all these and the oldest three Tilby males, however, Chester's only enemy was Mrs. Fritzwilla Sudsup, a widow who happened to live next door.

She became Chester's opponent simply because the goose dearly loved to eat flowers.

One Saturday evening in July while Hank and Lois were out on their almost weekly date and the four children were seated at the dinner table, the telephone rang. Steve answered, and as he listened silently, his face turned white and then red. Travis, watching his older brother intently, felt a strange premonition of trouble. The voice on the phone was that of a woman, and even from where Travis sat it was easy to tell that she was angry.

The conversation ended abruptly. Steve placed the phone carefully onto the receiver, pulled an ugly face at it, and turned toward Travis.

"Boy, Trav," he said, doing his best not to grin. "Is she ever mad. You're really in for it!"

"Who?" Travis asked, his eyes wide with surprise.

"Mrs. Sudsup. That's who!"

"Oh, no!" Jason groaned in mock horror as he threw his hands into the air. "Have us horrible Tilbys done it to her *again*?"

"Mrs. Sudsup," Jenni added as she rolled her own eyes. "She's yucky!"

"Steve," Travis groaned, "I haven't even been near her place, not for a week!"

"Well," Steve grinned, doing his best to control his own mirth (for he considered Mrs. Sudsup a busybody, and she was definitely not on his "ten most favorite persons" list), "if you weren't there in person, then you were there by proxy."

"What? What does *that* mean?"

"It means you were represented by someone else, dumb-dumb."

"Travis isn't a dumb-dumb," Jenni interrupted. "You are!"

"Back off, Jen, or I'll make you go to bed."

The little girl closed her mouth, crossed her arms tightly, and gave her oldest brother a look that would have made an icicle feel feverish. Travis looked at her, winked, and then turned back to Steve, anxious to learn what it was that could possibly have caused such a pile of trouble.

"Okay," the boy replied to Travis's further questioning, "here it is. That 'horrid, filthy' one-legged goose of yours has just eaten the blossoms off Mrs. Sudsup's award-winning flowers. You know, the flowers she's been bragging about to Mom every day since last May?"

Well, there was sudden hilarity in the Tilby kitchen. Jason cheered, Jenni clapped her hands, and all of them in general acted pretty much like you'd expect four kids to act after they've learned that their favorite bad guy, the one they love most to hate, has just lost to Superman again.

This isn't meant to say that the Tilby kids were bad, for they really weren't. It was just that Mrs. Sudsup, bless her minuscule heart, was an awfully difficult neighbor. She was as filled with pride as Chester, though she denied it and the goose didn't. Yet she disdainfully called the Tilbys shiftless and "renters"; she marked on the calendar each time that Hank brought home a new car (even though it was a company car, of course, provided by his job, for he could never have afforded one himself); she criticized and yelled at each of the children whenever they approached her fence; and she counted the hours that Lois spent in the yard playing with her family instead of doing "productive" things.

In addition, she told Lois frequently of the times when she had been forced to protect Lois and Hank's good name against the slanderous attacks of other neighbors (attacks, incidentally, which were never made manifest to Lois or Hank by any person other than good Mrs. Sudsup). And finally, she never ceased reminding Lois of the indisputable fact that her own lovely garden was thoroughly downgraded by the obviously feeble efforts of her neighbors. And somehow, no matter how Lois said it, Mrs. Sudsup could never understand that the Tilbys were raising people, not plants, in their yard.

Well, the kids were still laughing when they heard the sound of tires coming into the driveway. Suddenly Travis thought of Chester and of what was likely going to happen to him. Frantically he looked at Jason and Steve, hoping for help from them, but they just shrugged their shoulders and grinned. *Chester*, he thought as he rose to his feet, *what am I going to do with you?* And then his parents walked through the doorway.

For a long moment that house was as quiet as a tree full of owls at noontime, and then once again pandemonium broke loose. All four young people tried to tell about Chester at the same time, and anyone with kids can imagine what *that* sounded like. Finally, though, Hank managed to quiet them down.

"All right, Steve," he said, "tell it to me slow, and the rest of you kids stay quiet until he's finished."

Steve did so, sparing nothing, and the look on Hank's face grew darker and darker. Travis, glancing upward through his lashes, knew that Chester was in real trouble, and the boy almost died with fear. They couldn't kill Chester! They just couldn't!

And then Travis became aware of his mother. She seemed to be choking on something, for she was gasping and holding her face and doing all in her power to get her breath. In silence she struggled, and finally, when she could endure it no longer, she dropped her hands to her sides and . . . and *laughed*!

Travis could not believe it. His mother was laughing, holding her arms around herself and laughing until she could hardly breathe. And then suddenly, so, too, was his father. He was followed by Jason and Steve, and soon the entire family was racked with laughter, a crazy laughter which only increased the more they tried to get it under control.

Anyway, Travis was just starting to relax regarding his goose when Lois, gasping, jumped to her feet and stared out of the window.

"Well, of all the nerve!" she suddenly stormed, her smile disappearing instantly.

"Lois," her husband asked, surprised, "what is it?"

"Hank, look at that! Mrs. Sudsup is chasing poor Chester down the street with her broom. Why, I'm of a mind to . . ."

"Lois, relax. She has every reason to not only chase that goose but to brain it if she can catch it."

"She does not! Flowers can be replaced, Hank,

but how do you replace something as wonderful as Chester?"

"Wonderful? Lois, that goose is becoming the biggest . . ."

". . . *friend* Travis has," the woman concluded quickly. "Now, Hank, are you going to sit there arguing with me while that woman abuses our property, or am *I* going to have to take a stand?"

"*Our* property? For crying out loud, that feathered pest belongs to Mr. Larson."

"Of course it does. But he's asked Travis to raise it, and isn't Travis ours?"

"Well, yes. But . . ."

"Very well, Hank. If Chester is Travis's responsibility, and Travis belongs to you, then it's clear as crystal that Chester is also yours. Now, Mrs. Sudsup is doing her very best to damage your property. Don't you think you ought to get out there and stop her?"

Frustrated by his wife's logic, and still trying to remove the grin from his face, Hank hurried out of the front door to confront and hopefully placate the irate Mrs. Sudsup. Travis, relieved, was just starting to smile when his mother turned on him, her face suddenly stern.

"Now, young man, how many times have I told you to keep Chester tied up?"

"Mom, I can't put a rope around the only leg he has. It's not fair."

"Neither is it fair for him to eat Mrs. Sudsup's lovely flowers! Travis, if you don't want Chester's mortal existence to be terminated posthaste, you'd better come up with an idea of how you will keep him penned, and you'd better do it fast. That rope is just not good enough!"

Travis and Jenni looked at each other, each of them somehow knowing what was coming. At first Travis had been allowed to keep Chester in his room, but that had ended when the goose strutted into his parents' bedroom and hopped onto his father's stomach. Even that wouldn't have been so bad, except that Hank had been asleep, and Chester had awakened him by tweaking his nose with his beak. That had ended Chester's sojourn in the house. Now, after this episode, the goose would be even more restricted.

And so for the first time in his young life Chester found himself tied up tightly, the rope to remain in place until a pen was built. Travis didn't like doing it, Chester didn't like having it done and went to work immediately on the knot, and Jenni, when she watched the goose's frantic efforts to free himself, cried. But that was the way it was, and nobody could do anything about it.

There was also a family council held late that night, and the topic of discussion was the family's reaction to Mrs. Sudsup and her horticultural catastrophe. It was all understandable, Hank pointed out, but it was still wrong for them to laugh at another person's distress.

Lois then apologized to the children for her part in that laughter, and promised them that at church in the morning she would also apologize to Mrs. Sudsup. Travis was then told that he, too, was to apologize to Mrs. Sudsup, and though he groaned at the idea, once it was done he felt better about it.

Together, then, Hank and Lois told their children all they knew about their lonely neighbor, and they pointed out several possible reasons for Mrs. Sudsup's unfriendly behavior. They told of her childlessness, of the untimely death of her husband, of the fact that she had no family anywhere at all; and they spoke especially of her flowers, which had become her entire and only life—the very flowers that Chester had destroyed.

Needless to say, the children gained a new understanding of their neighbor; and by the time they all went to bed the entire family was not only feeling sorry for Mrs. Sudsup but was also vowing to try to make life more pleasant for her.

The single exception to that, of course, was Chester, who was tied up outside and so missed out on the conversation. That wayward bird had no thought of repentance, no thought at all. He also carried his hatred long and deep, and he never forgot an enemy. All of that, plus the fact that the goose was still working on the knot that Travis had tied, added up to trouble, and that is trouble with a capital T.

Chapter 8
Chester Goes to Church

The morning after the Sudsup episode was Sunday; and Travis, remembering the warnings of his mother and father, before leaving for church made certain Chester was still tied. The trouble was that Travis didn't check closely enough. During the night Chester had become proficient at knot picking, and Travis hadn't been gone fifteen minutes before the big goose at last worked the knot loose. And then, for the very first time in his life, Chester followed the unsuspecting Tilby family to church.

Travis, seated with his family in the chapel, was blithely unaware that Chester had decided to expand his spiritual horizons. However, Mrs. Sudsup, habitually late, could have enlightened Travis considerably on the subject. Or at least she could have if she had been given the opportunity. But she wasn't; she didn't; and so the first indication Travis had of Chester's sudden religious inclination came during the most quiet part of the meeting.

At that moment there erupted from outside the most horrible shriek Travis had ever heard—a shriek that quickly became part of a most unholy and un-Sabbath-like chorale.

Instantly all heads turned to stare, some of the old patriarchs creaked to their feet and hobbled out to render heroic assistance, and Travis, after one short glance at the horrified expressions on the faces of his parents, ducked his head in mortification and fear. He recognized that noise, that strange clicking and hissing, and he knew what was causing it.

"Chester," he whispered frantically to himself, "what are you doing *here*?"

As the old men filed out the door and joined the fracas, the noise, if anything, grew louder. The service came to a sudden halt, all around him people were whispering unanswered questions, and once or twice in the next sixty seconds Travis almost fled.

But he didn't, and then it was forever too late. His mother, her eyes flashing fire, suddenly leaped to her feet, pushed her husband back down, signaled stiffly for Travis to follow, and then marched down the aisle and out through the chapel door. Travis, wishing he were either dead or invisible, stood up and shuffled along behind her. And as he walked he did his best to ignore the staring and giggling of the other kids.

Mrs. Sudsup, by the time Travis and his mother had reached the door, was still screaming. She obviously had come late, and just as obviously had run into the same unforgiving goose which only the day before had been forced to flee before her rage and her broom. She, quite possibly, had forgotten the incident. Chester most definitely had not.

Without warning he had sighted the enemy, spread his huge wings, dropped his head into a charging stance, filled his chest with air, hissed loudly, and launched his surprise attack!

Poor Mrs. Sudsup must have felt like Pearl Harbor in December of 1941. She was bombed and strafed by a determined enemy, and the poor woman didn't have a chance. Instantly she was bowled over onto the ground, and by the time Travis and his mother got to her, which was perhaps only sixty seconds later, she had been pummeled and battered not only by the goose but by the misdirected swings of the old patriarchs' canes. Thus, when Travis first saw the poor woman, she was sitting in a decidedly unladylike posture in the middle of the sidewalk—her hat on the ground beside her, her fists clenched and shaking, and her emotions in a definite state of disrepair.

Chester, the undisputed victor of this unholy crusade, was hopping all about her, ignoring the old men and continuing to thrust his head in and out in a constant effort to further diminish the lady's self-righteous aplomb. In his bill was Mrs. Sudsup's wig, which no one was supposed to know about, and Chester was shaking that almost-living mop of synthetic hair and hopping about doing a virtual war dance, exhibiting just as much pride as any warrior had ever shown as he waved his first bloody scalp in the air and circled about some primitive campfire.

For what seemed forever, no one moved, and Travis had time to see and mentally record everything Chester had done to his neighbor. He saw that one shoe was off Mrs. Sudsup's foot; he saw the gaping holes in the woman's nylon hose; he saw the hairpins which had once been so neatly in place beneath the wig on her head, but which were now hanging in little ringlets down into her face; he saw her eyes bulging with fear and anger; he saw her tonsils quivering as she vainly tried to articulate her distress and wrath.

And then finally Travis's mother came back to life. She didn't say anything, for words seemed totally unfitting. Instead she merely pointed with her shaking finger, and Travis jumped. In one dive he was off the porch, had Chester in his arms, and was fleeing toward home, his mind filled with the vision of Mrs. Sudsup. He could also see his mother gazing with stricken dismay at her neighbor, who had been humiliated before her. And both those visions, as anyone might guess, were enough to give the boy tremblings of horror all the way home.

Once there, he immediately retied his goose to the tree, and was wondering what to do next when Jason loped up. He explained to Travis that he had cut out of church to get his little brother's ox out of the mud. Travis grinned weakly, and the two of them went to work.

Within an hour they had nailed a frame together and had covered it with old chicken wire. Chester, definitely disgruntled by the arrangement, was nevertheless lodged safely within the pen by the time the rest of the family arrived.

Another interesting family meeting was then held, the second in as many days; some firm ground rules were established; Chester remained among the living; Travis made another trek to Mrs. Sudsup's home to apologize; Lois called Mrs. Sudsup on the telephone, apologized profusely, and invited the neighbor woman to come over in the morning for a pleasant social visit. Mrs. Sudsup somewhat reluctantly accepted, and all in all things appeared to be working out surprisingly well.

And then it started to rain.

Chapter 9
The Hamper

There's nothing like a rainy day in the summer to put a person out of sorts, especially if that person is a thirteen-year-old boy with a pet goose outside who seems to be drowning. Now, everyone knows that a goose is a waterfowl and so isn't bothered by rain. However, such knowledge didn't help Travis at all. He could see Chester, he could see the steadily drizzling rain, and the poor goose honestly looked miserable. Consequently Travis was miserable as well, and anyone ought to be able to understand that.

For an hour or so the boy sat at the kitchen window, staring out through the streaked and wetly wavering glass, watching his pet. The rain was not torrential, but it was steady, and through it all Chester did not move. He stood on his one foot, his head tucked back beneath a wing, and suffered patiently and in silence. Or at least that's how it looked to Travis.

"Mom," he wailed, "look! The poor thing's drowning."

Lois, busy baking cookies for Mrs. Sudsup's visit, patiently walked to the window and looked.

"Yes," she said, "it certainly is raining. I'll bet Chester just *loves* it. He's had too little water in his life, especially since he's a goose. This will do him a world of good."

"Mom!"

And Lois, smiling at her son, returned to her baking.

Jenni, too, was suffering that morning, for there is nothing like a rainy day in the summer to bring out the boredom in a child.

"Mom," she wailed, "what can I do? I'm *bored*!"

"Go play school, honey," Lois replied sweetly.

"I'm tired of school! I want to play something else."

"Then get out the crayons and color me a pretty picture."

"I don't want to color pictures. Mine are all ugly!"

"Then get a book and read it," Lois responded, her voice getting tighter.

"I don't want to read! That's *boring*!"

That sort of conversation went on until Lois, only human, had endured more than she was able. "Jenni," she finally snapped, "I don't care what you do. Just leave me alone and go do it!"

Then, angry with herself because she had become angry with her daughter, she returned to her baking, and Travis brought up the fact, once again, that poor Chester was drowning.

Finally Lois, already on edge because Mrs. Sudsup was due at any moment, turned from the sink and confronted her children.

"That's enough!" she snapped. "I don't like the rain any better than you, but unlike you I don't have time to be bored about it. Now, you two find something to do, and I don't want to see you or hear you again until Mrs. Sudsup has gone. Do I make myself clear?"

Both children nodded, left the kitchen, and climbed the stairs to the boys' bedroom.

"Scrud!" Travis groaned as he stared down from his window at Chester. "What are we supposed to do? I'll bet Chester hates the rain. I'll bet Mom would hate it if she was out in it. Wish I could get him in here and hide him. Then—"

"Hey, Trav," Jenni interrupted excitedly, "I know what we can do."

"Yeah, me, too. Run away."

Jenni giggled. "No, silly. Let's play hide 'n' seek."

"Hide 'n' seek? Come on, Jen. I'm thirteen years old! Besides, two people can't play that, especially in the house."

"Can, too. I've done it lots. Me and Michelle do it all the time. You hide first and I'll be it and find you. Then we'll trade."

Well, the upshot of that conversation was that Travis was stuck. He couldn't think of a nice way of telling Jenni no, so he ended up playing hide 'n' seek with his little sister. Meanwhile the rain continued to fall, and the day got more soggy and gloomy than ever—almost setting the stage, you might say, for what was coming.

A little later Travis was hunting for Jenni in the attic when he heard Chester raise a ruckus outside. At that same moment the doorbell rang, and Travis found himself grinning. He knew that Chester still recognized Mrs. Sudsup. Seconds later he heard her voice, rather high-pitched, and he grinned even wider, for he knew she hadn't forgotten, either. Those two, he decided, were pretty evenly matched, and he'd do well to avoid her, let Chester alone, and remove himself from the conflict entirely.

"Jen," he shouted. "Behind the trunk! I see your hand."

There was a brief hesitation, then suddenly Jenni jumped up. "Waaagh!" she screamed. "Scared you, I bet."

Inwardly Travis groaned. "Sure," he said, "you scared me to death. In fact, I think my heart's stopped."

Jenni giggled. But abruptly she stopped while her eyes widened with excitement. "Trav, I know what we can do. Pick a *really* good hiding place, and then, just before I find you, jump out and *scare* me. Okay?"

"I don't know, Jen," he replied wistfully. "I'm tired of this game."

"Please, Trav," she wailed, clasping her hands together. "Just this once? Please? Pretty, pretty please?"

Travis looked at his little sister and grinned once

again at her theatrics. She'd probably grow up and be an actress and be rich and famous and all that dumb stuff. Then he'd be glad he was her friend, more even than now, probably.

"Okay, Jen, but just this once more. And count to a hundred this time. I'm going to find a really good place to hide."

Jenni quickly agreed and immediately started counting. Travis bounced down the stairs, took a quick look through the bedrooms, decided he'd used all the good places there, and descended quietly to the main floor.

As he looked around he could hear the murmur of voices coming from the living room, and in his mind he could see his mother and Mrs. Sudsup. His mother was trim and pretty and usually calm and relaxed. Mrs. Sudsup, on the other hand, was dumpy and haggard and almost always looked like she was living on the ragged edge of life.

Of course his mother had pointed out that he and Chester were to a great extent responsible for the neighbor lady's recent obnoxious behavior; and though Trav couldn't quite see that, he still respected his mother's opinion. She'd told him to keep quiet and out of sight so Mrs. Sudsup would have no further reason for complaint, and he wasn't about to do otherwise. Not on his life he wasn't. That was why, as he looked for a hiding place, he tiptoed through the carpeted hallway. A confrontation with his mother, and probably his father, too, when he found out about it, was the last thing he needed.

But where to hide? Where would be a good place

that Jen wouldn't think of, where he could relax a little?

And then Travis saw, in the bathroom, the large clothes hamper his father had just purchased. "Ha," he whispered, grinning. "The perfect place to hide from my pesky little sister."

On an impulse he opened the hall cupboard, quickly located the large box containing Halloween costumes, pulled out his father's hideous rubber pirate mask, and quickly closed the cupboard. Slipping into the bathroom, he lifted the lid of the hamper and climbed inside. Thankful for once that he was small, he settled himself into the pile of soiled clothing and lowered the lid.

Struggling in the confined space, he finally managed to pull the grotesque mask over his head, and then he grinned as he thought of how he looked. The mask's hideous features, tortured expression, and gash of shiny red were perfect, and Jenni would get the scare of her innocent young life. Of that he was certain.

"She'll take a long time to find me," he breathed at last. "I might as well relax and enjoy this."

Suiting thought to action, Travis closed his eyes and began thinking again of ways to get his goose to fly. Time passed, he grew sleepy, dozed a little, wondered where Jenni was that it was taking her so long, and was just thinking of getting out and ending the silly game when he heard her come quietly into the bathroom.

Instantly Travis stilled his breath. He couldn't make anything out through the small eye openings in the mask and the tiny openings in the wicker hamper, so he waited, his breath stilled, wondering how he could scare her without upsetting his mother and Mrs. Sudsup, who were still in the next room.

Then suddenly the door to the bathroom closed, and Travis grinned. Jenni knew where he was, and she was smart enough to close the door so his growl and her squeals wouldn't be heard outside the room. Well, that was great. It certainly solved the problem. Now she ought to be opening the lid, and he would jump up with a howl and scare the daylights out of her.

But she didn't, and Travis couldn't understand why. He could hear her moving around, quietly, so quietly. Was she teasing him, making him wait while she set herself? Knowing Jenni, that was probably what she was doing, all right. She was getting ready, and was going to try and scare *him*.

Well, he thought determinedly, *that isn't going to work. No, sir, it isn't! I'll throw the lid back, jump out, and frighten the heck out of her before she has a chance to do it to me. That'll get her!*

Quietly, almost totally silently, Travis tensed his muscles and pulled his legs under him. Then he reached up, placed his hand on the underside of the lid, and was ready.

With a final grin of anticipation he slammed open the lid, sprang to his full height, raised his hands over his head in a menacing posture, growled hideously into the quivering rubber of the mask—and found himself almost knocked backward by the force of an ear-piercing scream.

Ripping off his mask, Travis gaped around, and

to his horror he found that Jenni was nowhere in sight. Instead he found himself gazing upon Mrs. Sudsup, her eyes bulging out, her face the embodiment of terror, her body doing its best to back off from the one seat in the house from which there was no backing off, and her screams creating a strident threat to his suffering eardrums.

Travis never did remember getting out of the hamper, nor could he recall much of his and Mrs. Sudsup's almost simultaneous exits from the bathroom. He did remember, however, a portion of her departing speech, and even though it was a remarkably creative appraisal of his personality and likely destiny, he would never have repeated those things to anyone. Ever!

Travis's horrified mother watched the woman's unceremonious exit, too, and though she didn't know all of what had happened, she did know that it again concerned her youngest son. She knew, too, that Mrs. Sudsup had her suds up once more, so to speak, and that whatever progress the apologies of Travis and herself had made in winning her neighbor was now undone.

Slowly she turned to glare at her son; and Travis, as anyone can understand, was dying inside. Again.

Chapter 10
An Unexpected Ally

One of the things that made life so difficult for Travis that summer was that his older brothers were growing up. They weren't grown up yet, of course, not by a long shot, but their hormones were stirring fairly briskly; and Hank was fond of saying that his two sons reminded him of raw nerve endings looking for rough places to grate against.

Travis didn't really understand that, of course. All he knew was that Jason and Steve were suddenly interested in things that had no meaning for him at all, and more and more he was feeling left out.

Jason, who was at last sixteen, had in Travis's opinion gone especially dippy. He had a severe case of Sheryl-Hanson-on-the-brain, and though he still had not spoken *to* her at all, she was all he could ever think or speak *of*.

Steve, though not old enough to date, was surely old enough to be a spectator, as he continuously and rather mischievously pointed out; and he enjoyed spectating every bit as much as Jason did. In fact, Steve was head over heels "in like" with a new girl every other day, though *he* hadn't spoken with very many of them, either. But night after night the two older brothers would lie in bed talking about girls, describing them, discussing them, anguishing over them, trying to understand them, and scheming up ways of getting "wheels" so they could make time with them. And all the time poor Travis was groaning inwardly, wondering how two guys who had been so smart could so suddenly have all their gears stripped.

"I'm telling you," Jason would whisper to Steve, "if I see Sheryl with Alec one more time, I'll die!"

"You really like her?"

"Oh, wow! She's the cutest little filly in the county, and I mean it! I just wish she was my girl."

"Why don't you cut Alec's grass?" Steve would ask, sounding disgusted. "Take her out. You're old enough now, you lucky crumb. She'd probably like you better than that creep Suggins, anyway."

"Are you kidding? She'd never even talk to me. Scrud, I don't even have a car. What would I take her out on? The tractor?"

Steve would snicker, Jason would get upset, and then Travis would make his often repeated statement, which seemed to irritate both brothers to an amazing degree. "I don't see why a car's such a big deal," he'd say. "Or girls, either, for that matter!"

He'd say that, and both older boys would groan with the agony of spirit which their little and very immature brother caused them.

"Well, I don't," Travis would repeat, defending himself. "I've got to have help if I'm going to get Chester to fly before Thanksgiving, and all you guys do is talk about girls. It's dumb! Why don't you talk about something important?"

And then the wrath and derision of both Jason and Steve would descend upon him like the plagues of Moses, almost withering Travis with their force. Angry and hurt, he would roll over and close his eyes and ears while the conversation of his brothers turned to beautiful cars and ways to get the same in order to get even more beautiful girls.

Travis, however, even as he was going to sleep each night, would still find himself wondering why cars were necessary to get real girlfriends, and even why his brothers wanted girlfriends at all. He wondered, but he spent little time worrying about it, for he had more important things to consider.

One day late in July, when his brothers were both working in the second crop of hay for Mr. Larson, Travis decided to take Chester swimming. He thought about two or three places, but finally decided upon Les Simms's pond, which was nicest and deepest, and which was where the older kids usually swam. That day, however, the pond was deserted, and Travis and his goose had it to themselves.

Gleefully Travis dove and swam beneath the surface, the coolness washing over his body and relaxing him like nothing else could. For a few moments he swam rapidly, diving and surfacing and even chasing fish, though he never got anywhere near their fleeting forms. Finally exhausted, he rolled onto his back and kicked to where Chester was swimming in large circles, doing his best to swim straight.

"Boy," he gasped as he pushed the goose straight through the water, "you've got a real problem, Chester. You not only can't fly, but you can't even swim. What kind of a dumb waterfowl are you, anyway?"

Chester, seeming to understand, turned and grabbed Travis's nose with his bill, the boy was instantly submerged, and seconds later, coughing and gasping and laughing, the goose and his master were locked in a struggle to see which could more quickly drown the other.

For a few moments the game continued, back and forth across the pond, with Travis first pushing the goose and then pulling him. At last, too tired to swim any longer, he crawled out onto the grassy shore and flopped onto his back. Chester, hopping out after him, ruffled his feathers, preened for a few moments, and then began hopping up the bank in search of a few bugs for lunch.

"Chester," Travis said as he watched the long silky neck darting after nourishing treasures, "what am I going to do? You're plenty big enough to fly, only you can't, and I don't know how to teach you. But you've got to learn! You've just *got* to! I can't let Mr. Larson kill you for Thanksgiving. And

93

he will, too, if you aren't gone. He means business, Chester. He's rich, and he gets what he wants. *Nobody* argues with Mr. Larson!"

The afternoon sky was dotted with marshmallow clouds, and Travis was lying there thinking of them and of ways to get his goose up into them and away from Mr. Larson. Gradually Travis became aware of the sound of an approaching car. Sitting up, he realized that Chester had hopped off on some business of his own, and Travis had no idea where the bird had gone.

Scrambling up the bank and looking for Chester so he could get out of there, Travis was horrified to see, almost at the pond, a red convertible (one he had seen frequently as it roared past his home) filled with laughing teenagers.

Alec Suggins! The bully!

Travis instantly ducked down, feeling the strange fear that was suddenly balled into the pit of his stomach. He couldn't let Alec see him! Not here, not when he was alone. Alec would tear him apart, and Travis knew it. He also knew that it wasn't done because Alec hated him; the older boy didn't, or at least that was what Jason had said. Alec picked on Travis because that was the best way he could find of getting at Jason, who simply ignored Alec's taunts otherwise. *Oh*, Travis thought, *if only Jason were here.*

But then it was too late. Alec had seen him, and was now standing on top of the bank leering down at the crouching Travis.

"Well, well," he laughed, his masculine voice filled with derision. "Hey, you guys, come up here and look at this. I've got a little gopher cornered down in its hole."

"A gopher?" some girl squealed excitedly. Within seconds the top of the bank was crowded with ten kids, all of whom had planned on going swimming.

"Oh, Alec," another girl giggled, "he's not a gopher. He's too cute to be a gopher."

"Maybe he's a flower," some boy said. "A pretty flower. He's rooted there, and he's sure shaking in the breeze."

"Then he's a tree," another shouted. "A quakie. Quakies shake even when there isn't a breeze."

Everyone laughed, and then Alec jumped down the bank toward Travis, shouting "Boo" as he did so. Startled by the sudden move, Travis staggered backward, tripped over a tree root, and sprawled on the ground.

"Yeah," Alec shouted while the others laughed, "he's a quakie, all right, but he's not rooted very good. No strength, I guess. Hey, Tilby, you still climbing ropes?"

Travis silently rose to his feet, unsure of what to do or of how to get away. He could feel his face burning with embarrassment, and he was dying a thousand deaths knowing that all those girls were watching him.

"Sheryl," Alec continued, "this is the rope-climbing champion of the world. He climbs big long three-foot ropes in record time. You should see him. It's a riot!"

"Alec," Sheryl said quietly, "I don't think—"

"Neither does he," Alec continued, interrupting the girl as he picked up her thought. "In fact, none

95

of the Tilbys think very well, especially that crumb Jason. That's why they're always so poor. Ain't that right, Tilby!"

Travis was so angry by then that he was shaking, and as he fought to control himself he realized that he really was like a quakie, which was not funny at all.

"Hey, Alec," another called, "do you think if I took off my belt and tied it to this milkweed that Tilby'd give us climbing lessons?"

"Yeah," another laughed, "he's the one who was going to show us how *not* to do it."

"You guys," Sheryl stormed, "I think you're being mean!"

"Relax, Sheryl," Alec laughed, "we're just having a little fun. Hey, Tilby, where's that wimpy big brother of yours?"

"He ain't—isn't wimpy, you creep!" Travis shouted, no longer able to keep still. "If he was here, you'd be in big trouble."

"Oh, wow, a real bad guy, huh? I'm so scared I'm shaking."

"Me, too," echoed two or three others, their words filled with derision. "He's making us quakies, too!"

"Listen, little wimp," Alec said, "you go home and tell big brother wimp his mommy needs to wipe his nose. Now, run along, and don't get the lace on your underwear dirty."

There was another howl of laughter, but Travis was beyond hearing or even worrying about that. His anger was so intense that his reason snapped, and with a snarl that was half shout and half sob he launched himself at the older and much larger boy.

For an instant Alec stepped back, surprised, while Travis pummeled him with clenched fists. But then, grinning, he reached out and grabbed Travis's arms. "Come on, you guys," he gasped as he struggled to hold the wildly fighting Travis, "this wimp needs another swim to cool off."

Instantly several hands grabbed Travis, and within seconds he was swinging in the air, back and forth, even as he fought and shouted out his anger and frustration.

Suddenly he was released, and as he hurtled through the air toward the water Travis heard a surprised shout coming from the bank. He was aware briefly of a gray form launching itself into the group of teenagers. Then the waters of the pond swallowed him and he was going down and down, finally stopping and swimming desperately for the surface.

Gasping for breath, he cleared his eyes and only then realized that Chester had taken up the cause of the Tilbys where Travis had left off. There was a melee on the bank, with a lot of shouting and jumping around; and the big goose was in the middle of it, hissing and puffing and stabbing at anybody who seemed most handy. Girls were screaming, boys were grunting and yelling as they swung with their fists and kicked with their feet, and through it all hopped and fluttered Chester, a tireless warrior striking in defense of his water-treading prince.

Suddenly there was an extra loud yell, and Alec

tumbled out of the crowd, swinging and fighting at the monster that had attached itself to his ear. With a cry of pain he crawled toward the water, still fighting; and Travis, suddenly grinning, struck out for shore. But within seconds another boy, a heavy stick in his hand, was standing above the goose, readying himself to swing whenever he had a good shot.

"No!" Travis screamed as he flailed at the water. "Noooooooo!"

But it was too late, for the stick suddenly descended and with a sodden thud smashed against the body of the goose. Chester jerked, released Alec's ear, and rolled onto his side. The stick was in the air and descending once more when Travis, finally on the bank, dived beneath it and covered the goose with his body.

Whump! The heavy stick jarred against his ribs, smashing at his wind, and Travis blanched with the pain.

"Kill it!" one or two kids were shouting as hands tugged to pull Chester away from the boy. "Get the kid out of the way and kill that crazy bird!"

Travis, too sore and winded to cry out, clung fiercely to his pet, doing his best to shield it from further blows. But there were too many hands, he could feel the goose slipping away, and he was powerless to prevent the attack.

"Stop it!"

The feminine voice was shrill and powerful, and instantly all activity ceased. Travis, looking up, was startled to see Sheryl Hanson standing there, her hands clenched at her sides, her face white with anger. Without hesitation the girl reached out, took hold of Alec's arm, and jerked him away from Travis and Chester. Moving quickly, she pulled a couple more kids away, and then gently, silently reached down and helped Travis to his feet. Only then did she turn and speak again to the crowd.

"You make me sick," she said disgustedly. "Every one of you! What kind of people are you, anyway, picking on kids? Now, go on. Get out of here and leave this boy alone!"

"But, Sheryl," Alec pleaded, "it wasn't our fault. We were just teasing, and then this crazy goose . . ."

"Teasing," Sheryl snapped. "Do you think Travis felt like it was teasing?"

"I don't know, but big deal! We didn't mean anything. Big kids pick on little kids all the time. It happened to us and now it's our turn to do the picking. Now, come on. We'll let the little wimp and his stupid goose go, and then we can go swimming."

"Are you crazy, Alec? I wouldn't go swimming with you if my life depended on it. In fact, I'll never go anywhere with you again! Ever! Period!"

"Oh, yeah? How you going to get home?"

"I'll walk!"

Alec, shocked by the sudden turn of events, tried to laugh, couldn't, and turned angrily toward his car. "Come on, you guys. If she wants to stay with that stupid wimp, fine. Let's go and have some fun."

After the others had gone, Travis examined Chester, who did not seem to be badly hurt. Sheryl stood silently, watching but saying nothing; and it seemed to Travis that she was as uncomfortable as he was. And he *was* uncomfortable. Though he didn't like to admit it, he had noticed girls a little, and he was terrified of them. Sheryl of course was older, but she was still a girl, she was every bit as pretty as Jason had said she was, and she was also the first girl outside his family that he had ever been alone with. It was more than frightening, it was . . .

"Is he okay, Travis?"

Dumbly Travis nodded, not daring even to look up at her. How did she know his name? he wondered. He'd never talked to her, never even been close to her.

"I . . . I'm sorry we hurt your goose," she said quietly. "I'm even more sorry that we hurt you."

"It's okay. I ain't . . . I'm not hurt."

He'd have said more, but his brain was as dry as his mouth, and he could think of nothing except how nervous he was. Suddenly Sheryl was sitting beside him in the grass, though, and he wanted to run, to get away from her.

"What's its name?"

"Huh?"

"The goose. Is it a boy or a girl goose, and what is its name?"

"This is Chester, and I think it's . . . he's a boy."

"Can I touch him?"

Gosh, Travis thought, *she sounds just like Jenni. Maybe all girls are alike, only some are just a little bigger than others.*

"Sure," he said, relaxing a tiny bit. "Geese like girls about as much as they do boys, I guess."

Sheryl giggled (again like Jenni, Travis thought), reached out, and gently touched Chester's long neck. For an instant the goose froze, but Travis clicked some nice thoughts to him and shortly the big bird relaxed.

"He's so *soft*, Travis. I've never touched a real wild goose before. I didn't know they felt like that. I . . . Oh, what happened to his leg?"

"He lost it when he was a baby. In a fire—at least I think so."

"What makes you think that?"

"Because he hates fire so much. When he was little, and even now that he's big, whenever we burn garbage we have to be sure he's penned up or else he goes crazy."

"Does it hurt him, do you think? The stump, I mean."

"Not with pain, I guess. But it hurts in other ways."

"What do you mean?"

Travis looked up at the girl who was seated beside him, wondering at her interest and at the fact that he was talking to her so easily.

"He can't fly," he answered quickly.

"But I don't understand."

Travis then explained about geese needing speed to fly, which they got by running rather than hopping, and Sheryl instantly understood and sympathized.

"I guess you don't mind if I walk home with you?" she suddenly asked.

"Shucks, no," Travis said quickly as he rose to his feet. "We've got to be going, anyway, so I can work with Chester a little more before my brothers get home. Come on, goose, let's walk Sheryl home."

As they walked they talked, and it wasn't long before Travis felt as comfortable around Sheryl as he did around Jenni. He told her all about Chester and Mr. Larson and about how Thanksgiving was getting closer and about how he had tried everything he could think of and still Chester wouldn't fly. He told her about his parents and his brothers and about Mrs. Sudsup and about how much trouble he and Chester were always in; and Sheryl laughed delightedly as Travis related each incident. Travis then showed her how Chester enjoyed playing tag, and almost instantly Sheryl was running down the dirt road with Chester hopping along in full pursuit—she laughing heartily, Chester clicking for all he was worth, both enjoying the game equally.

Travis grinned and ran to catch up, and by the time they were nearly to Sheryl's home the three were like old friends, chatting and laughing and thoroughly enjoying each other's company.

"Trav," Sheryl suddenly asked as they neared her front gate, "can I ask you a question?"

"Sure."

"Don't laugh, okay?"

Travis grinned. "I won't laugh. What do you want to know?"

"Uh . . . does Jason like me?"

Looking up at her and determining that she was serious, the boy nodded. "I'll say," he declared soberly. "You're all he talks about. You and cars."

"Really?"

Now Travis looked at her again, for the tone of the girl's voice was definitely different, almost like she had discovered a great secret that she had known all along.

"Yep," he said simply. "Really."

"What does he say?"

"Oh, dumb stuff, mostly—like how he doesn't dare talk to you because you're Alec's girl and because he doesn't have a car, and about how much he wishes you were his girl instead of Alec's."

"Well, I'm *not* Alec's girl. But what does a car have to do with him talking to me?"

"Search me. He says all he has to take you out on is the tractor, and he thinks that'd be dumb. He says you'd think so, too."

"I would not! I think that'd be fun!"

"He sure doesn't think so. He says you're too special to take out on a tractor."

"Oh, that's sweet." Sheryl sighed, smiling happily. "But honestly, I *do* think a date on a tractor would be fun."

"Well, tell *him* that."

"Trav, I can't say something like that to Jason."

"Why not? You said it to me."

Sheryl smiled at the boy. "Yes," she said quickly, "but we're old friends. It's different with Jason and me. I've never even talked to him before, except to say hi at school. But I thought he didn't like me."

"Why?"

"Because he never answered me back."

"Gosh," Travis snorted, "he's so dumb. I guess it's just 'cause he's scared of you."

"But he doesn't need to be scared of me, Trav. I think he's cute."

"Well, don't let *him* hear you say that. *Cute* is a sissy word. He wants to be good-looking."

"That's what I meant," Sheryl responded quickly, smiling again.

"Do you want me to tell him?"

"What?"

"About the tractor. Do you want me to tell him that you'd like a date on it?"

"Oh, no! I mean, I don't think . . . uh . . . I mean . . . could you tell him without him knowing that I said it . . . I mean . . . uh . . . that I said it like I did . . . uh . . ."

Travis grinned, delighted to know that other people, especially girl people who were as pretty and nice as Sheryl, got embarrassed as easily as he did. And Sheryl was definitely embarrassed. Her face was red, and suddenly she wouldn't even look at him.

"Sure," he said quickly. "I'll figure out a way to tell him. Hey, do you want to come over and help me teach Chester to fly?"

"Could I? When?"

"Oh, anytime. Come over tonight, and Jason'll probably be there."

Sheryl grinned, winked boldly at him, told him that she would come if she could possibly do so, thanked him for walking her home, and said good-bye to Chester. Then she was gone and Travis was walking up the lane with Chester, more amazed than ever that a girl who was as old and pretty as Sheryl had actually talked and walked with him. It was neat! It was really, really neat, and he couldn't wait until he told Jason.

AUGUST

Chapter 11
A Snake in the Grass

The stream danced over the rocks, singing quietly, and sunlight glanced from the water. A few feet away it rippled and eddied quietly about a branch that was being pushed gently back and forth, while in the trees above, the leaves also danced in the cool morning breeze.

Travis sat contentedly, enjoying the quiet and letting it ease into his soul. To his ears came only the sound of water and the sound of wind in the pines across the narrow canyon, a far-off sound that, when he closed his eyes, seemed like cars swooshing along a distant highway late at night. Across the stream, not far off, two squirrels frisked busily about, and below him, in the trees, Chester was ducking his head repeatedly into the cold water of the creek.

It was the fourth and final day of their annual summer camp, the wonderful time when he, his father, and his brothers ventured alone together into the mountains. This year they were camped behind Mount Nebo, about five miles above Ockey's KOA ranch, and were enjoying the solitude of upper Salt Creek Canyon.

It had been a great week, and Travis was intensely sorry to see it come to an end. More than anything in the world he loved to be in the mountains, and he loved it especially when he was with his father and his older brothers. Going back, however, meant that he would have to face the prospects of school, which more than anything else meant Coach Gruninger, the laughter of the kids, and The Rope.

He'd made no progress on it at all, and he knew what was going to happen. Jason wouldn't be around because he was going to high school; Steve didn't care that much what happened to him; and Coach or the kids would get him again, sure as shooting. Travis dreaded that thought, and he agonized about it constantly.

Even more, though, he agonized about his goose, his dumb goose who wouldn't learn to fly. There were only three months left until Thanksgiving, and Travis was becoming desperate. He needed help with the goose, and he knew it. But nobody would help him. His father and mother were too busy, Jason and Steve just laughed at him, and he and Jenni and sometimes Sheryl simply couldn't do the job alone.

Travis grinned now as he thought of the day he had met Sheryl. It had been a pretty awful experience with Alec and the others, but he supposed it had been worth it, considering what had happened with Jason and Sheryl. In fact, when he closed his eyes, he could still see and hear Jason, who could neither comprehend nor accept the fact that Travis had actually met and spoken with the gorgeous and totally unavailable Sheryl Hanson.

"She *what*?" Jason had asked in surprise, his voice registering his disbelief. He was standing in the downstairs bathroom, stripped to the waist, doing his best to wash the hay dust from his face and body. But he was no longer washing, he was no longer doing anything at all except staring wide-eyed into the mirror. Travis was standing behind him, leaning against the doorframe, grinning.

"I said," Travis had repeated playfully, "Sheryl's coming over tonight to help me teach Chester to fly."

"Sheryl who?"

"Come on, Jason, don't be so thick. Sheryl who-do-you-think?"

"But . . . but why?" the older boy asked as he slowly turned around, dripping soap and water onto the floor. "How come she'd want to come here and . . . Oh, I get it. This is your dumb idea of a joke. Well, ha-ha-ha! It isn't funny."

Travis shrugged and continued grinning. "It isn't supposed to be funny," he replied easily. "It's just the truth. That's all. Of course, if you aren't interested . . ."

"Mom," Jason called out pleadingly, "is Travis telling the truth?"

Lois, at the stove, grinned. "How would I know?" she answered. "I can't hear what he's saying."

"Scrud," Jason growled "it's about Sheryl. You know."

"Oh, that," Lois replied, winking at Hank, who was seated at the table trying to concentrate on the paper. "Well, I suppose he is. He told me the same thing, and Trav never lies to me, at least that I know of."

"See?" Travis said.

"Well, then, how come she's coming here?"

"I told you—to help me teach Chester to fly."

Jason rolled his eyes in mental torment. "Sure," he said. "She's involved in charity work, and your dumb goose is one of her welfare projects."

"I don't know about that," Travis replied, still grinning. "I walked her back from Les Simms's pond today, and she happened to mention that she might come over tonight to help me."

"Come on," Jason responded doubtfully, "Les Simms's pond? What were you doing there?"

"Swimming."

"*Swimming?* You went swimming with *Sheryl*?"

"Well, yeah," Travis answered, suddenly feeling like he was on uncertain ground. "Something like that."

"Now I *know* you're lying," Jason snorted as he turned back to the sink. "I saw her with Alec this afternoon."

"She was, but she left him and came with me."

"Ha-ha-ha," Jason responded, scrubbing again.

"Okay," Travis replied, turning away. "But if she shows up, don't say I didn't warn you. I think she's probably more interested in seeing you than she is in seeing Chester."

Jason had sputtered and spun around once more. "Wha—what? What'd she say?"

"According to you, nothing," Travis answered. "According to you, I wasn't even with her."

"*Travisssss?*"

"Nope. I'm through talking. Just go ahead and stew in it now, and if she comes, you'll wish you'd talked a whole lot more nicely to your little brother."

"Mommmmmmmm!"

"I'm sorry, Jason," Lois answered sweetly. "But I really can't help you."

And that was the way it went. By the time Sheryl *did* show up, which actually surprised even Travis, Jason was fit to be tied. He tried to act nonchalant but couldn't, he tried to sound nonbelieving but couldn't, and he tried with all his heart to get Travis to tell him more, for deep down he wanted with all his heart to believe. In even that, however, he failed.

All through supper Travis grinned, and Jason only growled back. After supper, when Travis went out to work with Chester, throwing him into the air and trying to get him to spread his wings, Jason had gone into the front room and sprawled onto the couch with a magazine, doing his best to ignore what was going on outside.

And then Sheryl came. Travis doubted that he'd ever forget the look on Jason's face when the older boy, unable to restrain himself, came to the door a little later and saw the girl, who at that moment

112

was laughingly running from one of Chester's feigned attacks.

Travis, unusually quick with his tongue, spotted Jason and immediately shouted out: "Jase, Sheryl's here!" Jason, unable to duck, which he'd dearly wanted to do, stood lamely while Sheryl looked up, waved gaily, smiled, and shouted, "Hi, Jase." Then she turned away and went eagerly about her work with Chester.

Now, sitting on the bank of the stream, Travis thought of all that had happened since that day. Sheryl was more and more a part of the Tilby landscape, and Jason was even being more kind to him, probably because Sheryl treated him so kindly. But sadly, that was all that had changed.

Interest, at least on Sheryl's part, seemed to have shifted from Chester to Jason. Now, whenever she was around, she just stared at Jase with her big eyes. *Just like Gerty the cow*, Travis thought disgustedly. Besides that, Jason still didn't like Chester; Steve hadn't changed much; and his mother and father were even more reluctant to help, simply because of the principle of the thing.

"Trav," Hank and Lois had said on several occasions, "we can't feel good about what you are doing, let alone help you. You agreed to raise that goose for Mr. and Mrs. Larson so they could eat it, and now you are in effect trying to steal it from them. How can you ask us to support that?"

Travis couldn't, and deep down he knew they were right. But doggonnit, that didn't change how he felt inside. Chester was like his best friend, and he wasn't about to stand idly by and see the poor bird get stuffed and eaten, not by a long shot he wasn't! One way or another, he vowed, he would get Chester to fly away!

"Gosh," he groaned softly, speaking to his goose, who was still poking about in the creek. "If only Jase and Steve liked us, Chester. You'd like them if they'd just like you first. I know you would."

Lying back in the grass, Travis stared upward once more. Above him tiny puffballs of cloud sailed across the sparkling blue of the sky, and for a time he lay still, watching them pass. Then he watched a hawk as it drifted overhead, its lazy circles of flight carrying it slowly southward. It was moving in the same direction as the clouds, and when Travis shut all else from his mind, he could actually feel like he was floating along with the clouds and the hawk.

For as long as he could remember, Travis had wanted to fly, to see the earth drift by below him while the high wind currents carried him along. And he *had* flown. Once.

He'd been in a plane with his father and another man, Michael Hurst. And Mr. Hurst had turned the controls over to Travis. He had done well, too, for about thirty seconds. But then, as any nine-year-old boy might do, he had decided to climb. Not being a halfway person, he'd pulled the yoke clear to his chest; and the plane, a Piper Comanche, had gone straight into the air. Well, his father had yelled, Travis's cheeks had sagged, and he'd thought he was going to be shoved through the floorboards. Thoroughly frightened, he'd pushed the yoke all the way forward, the plane had looped over into a steep dive, and Trav and everyone else in the craft had suddenly become weightless. The dirt from the floor had been hanging in the air, a package had floated past, and Trav had been held down only by his seat belt. That part had been fun, really fun. It had also been extremely brief, for Mr. Hurst, his face white, had at that point grabbed control. Travis, understandably, had not flown since. Still he dreamed, and one way or another, he knew, he would someday fly again.

Suddenly, faintly, Travis heard the honking of a gaggle of Canadian geese, and he watched fascinated as their irregular "V" formation beat its way southward. The geese were flying much higher than the hawk, and in a short time they simply vanished from sight, disappearing into the blueness of the sky.

Again Travis thought of Chester, of how his own honker probably would never be up there with the other wild geese, flying freely to wherever he wanted to go; and Travis's heart immediately began to ache.

What could he do about it, though? How could he possibly help Chester learn to fly? And why did his life seem so wrapped up with flying?

For a time Travis simply dreamed, envying the freedom of the clouds, the hawk, and the geese. Oh, how he wanted Chester to be free, to be able to climb and soar and go where he wanted, letting the high-up winds carry him away from his troubles, away forever from Thanksgiving!

For a little while Travis even dreamed that *he* was soaring alongside Chester. In his mind he saw himself sailing along, fingertip to wingtip with his goose, looping and diving and climbing and soaring, free of everything, sailing in formation and finally landing gracefully in his front yard. There he stood humbly while his older brothers stared in awe and his father and mother hugged him and told him how proud they were to have such a gifted son and such a wonderful goose. Why, with him and Chester both able to fly, The Rope didn't matter anymore. Thanksgiving could come when it wanted, and nobody would ever make fun of either of them again. It was so wonderful . . .

But then suddenly the clouds dissipated and the hawk was gone, and Travis found himself right where he had always been, lying in the grass on the mountain and wishing that Chester's life and the camping trip would never end.

Later, when Travis went back to camp, he found his father taking a nap, and Jason and Steve gone. Travis, lonely and a little discouraged, sat down and began poking a stick into the fire.

What was wrong with the two of them? he wondered. Why couldn't he learn to climb the dumb rope, and why couldn't Chester learn to fly? If only Jase and Steve hadn't stopped teaching him. With their help he might have done it. And now they hated Chester—wouldn't help him; and it had only been after the most urgent pleading that Travis had been allowed to bring the goose on their camping trip. What was there about Chester that turned people away?

Travis's reverie was suddenly interrupted by the most fear-filled scream he had ever heard! Spinning, he saw Jason standing immobile about ten feet away, staring wide-eyed at the ground. Hank, too, was on his feet, speaking, his voice filled with an urgency Travis had never before heard.

"Don't move!" his father whispered as he moved a little closer to his son. "Whatever you do, Jase, don't move!"

"But, Dad," Jason responded, his voice a shaky whisper, "he struck my boot, and he's already coiled and ready to strike again! Do something, Dad! *Hurry!*"

Travis stared transfixed, aware for the first time of the constant angry buzzing. It was a rattlesnake, the biggest and ugliest rattlesnake he had ever seen—coiled less than a foot in front of Jason, its flat head raised and pulled back for another strike.

Hank Tilby, casting about for a weapon, suddenly saw his youngest son standing there.

"Trav," he called urgently, "find me a stick or a rock. Anything! And hurry!"

But then, just as Travis turned his gaze from the ugly triangular head of the snake, it struck at Jason again. And at that instant, as if from nowhere, a hissing, clicking, feathered monster smashed into the airborne rattler, knocking it sideways into the rocks and dust of the mountain, removing the danger so that Jason could jump clear.

Then, while a hopping angry Chester distracted the poisonous reptile, Hank Tilby directed his sons to get back. With a long stick Hank then began prodding the snake, which with vicious hissing and buzzing, began slithering away from the camp.

For about fifty feet Hank and Chester followed it, herding it along until at last it disappeared into the crevice of a rock.

Moments later, the reaction set in, and both Hank and his oldest son started to shake.

"Why didn't we kill it?" Steve suddenly demanded.

"I don't know," Hank answered quietly. "I didn't really think about it then, but I guess we didn't need to. It was only doing what came naturally."

"But, Dad, it's dangerous!"

"So are we, son."

"Not to us."

"Neither is it to it. Anyway, I think we did what was right."

Hank paused, looked back toward where he had last seen the rattler, and continued. "You know, that was far and away the biggest rattlesnake I ever saw. Even with the tail moving I counted over a dozen rattles, and the thing had to be three inches thick. It was huge!"

There was a chorus of agreement, then silence, and then a series of soft clicks made by Chester as he hopped up to Travis.

"Dad," Jason declared, "Chester saved my life."

"I know," Hank responded quietly. "I saw it."

"But why?" Jason questioned. "That dumb goose hates me!"

"No, he doesn't," Travis quickly declared. "He hates snakes. Them and fires. He also thinks you hate me, and so naturally he doesn't like you very much."

"I can't say that I blame him," Jason said quietly.

"Brother," Steve growled. "That dumb goose doesn't know enough to understand things like that! He's just a stupid—"

"Steve," Hank interrupted, "you're being negative again. That dumb goose, as you call it, just saved Jason's life. I think we ought not to judge any of God's creatures too harshly."

"Yeah," Jason declared quickly. "Chester, from now on, I call a truce. You and I are friends. Is that okay with you, Trav?"

Surprised, Travis quickly nodded and grinned at his older brother. Then they all began quickly packing, and it was only as they were leaving that Travis noticed the dark look on Steve's face—a look that told him of his brother's continued anger.

Chapter 12
To Teach a Bird to Fly

Of course, Jason's renewed friendship rekindled all of Trav's desires to teach his goose to fly, for finally he had real help once again. More than ever he was determined to see that prior to Thanksgiving Day it happened. To accomplish that, he set about giving the goose flying lessons. Or rather, he set about trying to. Trouble was, Chester didn't seem very anxious to become airborne.

Over and over Travis and Jason would throw the huge bird into the air, and over and over he would come flapping back to earth in an ungainly fashion, no more able to fly than your average washing machine or living room sofa. Chester simply would not, or could not, stay in the air.

Jenni and even Sheryl joined in, though Steve wouldn't; and The Rope was forgotten as they concentrated their free time and their energies on trying to teach Chester how to take to the sky.

Travis tried once or twice to get Steve to help as well, but Steve just turned away, and so Travis dropped it. Yet still he worried, for no one likes the feeling he has when another is angry with him.

Chester, though, was his main worry; and Travis spent all his thinking time trying to come up with a way to get the goose into the air. One day he even took the goose and, much to Chester's noisy protestations, climbed to the top of the barn with him. Then, with anxious approval from the others, he threw the hapless bird into the air.

For a moment (or at least an instant) it looked like Chester was at last going to do it. His wings were out, his foot was folded back, and even his tail feathers were spread. But then he didn't, and the sodden thud that came as Chester struck the earth so unnerved Travis that he refused to try that method again.

Jason and Jenni, of course, were there to pick Chester up, but Steve, who was standing nearby watching, laughed.

"I hope you killed him," he snickered. "Dumb thing won't ever fly."

"He will, too," Travis shouted angrily back.

"Won't, either, and you're just as dumb as the goose for thinking so."

"Go on, Steve," Jason responded quickly. "If you can't help us, go practice ball or something. Trav and Chester have enough troubles without you adding to them."

"Well, he *is* dumb, and you know it. He can't climb the rope, he can't catch a ball, he can't run very fast, he can't do anything. And he sure as heck ain't going to teach that stupid goose how to fly."

"Steve, get out of here! I mean it!"

"Who's going to make me?"

"I will, you little creep. One more word and I'll—"

"Jase," Travis interrupted, his eyes downcast. "It's okay. I don't care what he says. Besides, he . . . he's probably right."

"He is not!"

"I am, too," Steve snickered. "The poor little baby even says so himself. But don't worry, big brother. I'm going. I wouldn't stay around here if you begged me."

Steve gave his older brother a haughty look, snickered at Travis and Chester, ignored his little sister's angry glare, turned, and stalked off. And he was as unaware as any of the others that his mother had been standing at the side of the barn, listening.

"Steve," she called softly, still staying behind the barn.

The boy spun around in surprise, and Lois could tell from his guilty expression, which was quickly masked over, that he was certain she had heard him.

"Uh . . . hi, Mom," he gulped quickly.

"Steve, I'd like you to do something for me."

"Sure, Mom," he replied, suddenly hoping with all his heart that he had been wrong and that he wasn't in trouble at all.

"I'd like you to go to your room and spend the rest of the day there."

"But, Mom," he cried, his face showing innocent shock, "I didn't do anything! I . . ."

"Steve, no games. One argument and this will get a whole lot worse. I want you to spend this afternoon writing down all of the good things you can think of about Travis. Your father and I will look at your list tonight. I'd also like you to write down how you think my hearing what you said to Travis made *me* feel. Finally, I'd like you to say why you think I feel that way. Ten or twelve pages ought to do it. Do you understand me?"

Steve, his eyes downcast, nodded.

"Good. Now bend down so I can kiss you."

His expression showing his surprise at his mother's request, the boy nevertheless obeyed, turned, and trudged off toward the house. For a long moment Lois watched him go. Then, forcing a smile onto her face, she marched around the barn to where her other children were trying to teach Chester to fly.

"Travis," she said gaily, forcing a smile into her voice, "have you thought of letting other geese teach Chester?"

Travis stared at his mother without comprehension. But then, as it came, he realized that she was suddenly on his side, the world brightened, and suddenly nothing seemed impossible, nothing at all.

Chapter 13
Travis and His Mother

"Mom," Travis asked quietly, looking across the car at his mother, "are you sure this is going to work?"

"I don't know," Lois responded. "I hope it does. It's the only thing I can think of you haven't tried."

In the silence that followed, Travis focused his eyes on the road ahead. In front of them the headlights gobbled up the early morning darkness, and the boy thought again of Thanksgiving, which was getting closer all the time.

"Well," he stated finally, "it's got to work! It's just *got* to!"

Again there was silence, filled only with the whine of the tires on the road and the occasional soft clicking of Chester.

"Mom," Travis said suddenly, "I hope you don't get in trouble with Dad."

Lois looked over at her son, and despite her

worry she found herself smiling. He was such a delightful person, this little son of hers. He was thoughtful; his smile was contagious; and when he was happy, the whole world knew of it and soon grew happy, too.

"Sweetheart," she said gently, "husbands and wives don't get in trouble with each other. We're pretty close partners, you know. I'd have never done this if I hadn't talked with your father about it first, and he agreed that we needed to do something. After all, Chester seems to have become more than just a stray goose, at least as far as the Tilby family is concerned."

Lois paused, thinking, and then she continued. "Of course," she added wryly, "I did *not* consult with Mr. Larson, and in my opinion you should do that very soon. He needs to know how you feel about Chester."

Travis turned and looked at her; she winked, and the boy turned away, grinning.

Oh, if only Chester would fly! Lois thought as she felt her love for this boy swell within her. If he would, then Travis could relax; and she was certain the tension in the family would ease as well. And maybe this would do it, too, this crazy idea of hers. But all the while somehow she knew that it wouldn't. Somehow she knew.

"Where do I go?" she asked, forcing her mind away from her motherly fears.

"Down near the bottom of Lyn Rasmussen's lower field. Dad says he saw some wild geese there the other day, and Lyn told me last night when I called that they were still there."

Travis grew silent, and Lois looked at him again. He was so intense, so anxious about Chester.

"Mom," he said suddenly, "it's going to work."

"I hope so," she replied quickly. "But don't get your hopes too high. Maybe Chester isn't supposed to fly."

"But he *has* to, Mom. I've been teaching him wrong, I know I have. I don't know anything about flying. But geese do. If Chester sees them, then I'll bet anything he'll take off and fly with them. In fact, I—Chester, cut it out!"

Travis, squealing, pulled the goose's bill loose from his ear. Once he let go of Chester's head, however, Chester went for the ear again; and Lois, watching, felt again how much Travis loved his goose. Strangely she knew also that in his own way Chester loved Travis; and the fear within her suddenly grew. The goose was never going to fly.

Moments later she brought the car to a stop. "Do you want me to wait?" she asked.

Travis, already out of the car, with Chester in his arms, turned and looked at his mom. "Naw," he finally replied. "I can walk home. Besides, I won't have Chester to worry about. In a little while he . . . he'll be long gone."

Travis turned quickly away, embarrassed because of his emotions. "Thanks anyway, Mom," he gulped as he moved away. "See ya later."

Lois smiled through her own sudden tears, waited until Travis had climbed the fence and disappeared into the early morning darkness, and then she turned the car around and started home. But it wasn't going to work and she knew it, just as she knew that Travis would need her when it didn't.

With tears in her eyes she braked to a stop, turned off the engine, and waited, knowing what would happen and hoping with all her heart that she was wrong.

"Please," she whispered into the early morning darkness, "please help Chester to know how to fly. Please, dear God, Travis has hurt enough in his young life—with all of his sickness, with his hearing problems, with his bad eyes.

"Don't let him be hurt again by watching Chester fail, by watching him . . . die. I don't think I can stand seeing him suffer any more . . ."

And so, as the gray of dawn crept up over the East Mountain and spread quickly across Sanpete Valley, Lois Tilby tried to still the fear that was churning within her, the fear that her youngest son was once again going to be in pain. Ten thousand times more she would rather have suffered herself than to have Travis suffer, for as all mothers know, the pain of watching a child suffer is much harder on the mother than it ever is on the child.

Lois's own mother had once told her that, but she had doubted, and she had continued to doubt until her first son, Jason, developed pneumonia and nearly died. Interestingly Lois thought she was going to die, too—from exhaustion, from anxiety, and from vicariously suffering the pain that was racking the tiny body of her son. Only then had she understood and believed the words of her mother. And now she was suffering with Travis.

And though the pain was not physical, it was no less intense, no less real.

"Oh," she cried out through her quiet heartache, "what am I going to do? How can I ever, ever help him? Please, dear God, help me to know what to do."

Much later, long after the sun had come up, a visibly upset Travis trudged to the fence, climbed it, and slammed into the car. He was followed by a subdued Chester, who was missing whole clumps of feathers and who was speckled with blood.

Lois, after catching her breath at the sight, pulled out a box of tissues and began cleaning up both of them. Her heart and mind raced with questions and silent pleadings, but she said nothing and simply worked, knowing that when Travis was ready, he would speak.

"Mom," he finally said, his voice quiet with controlled anger, "those dang geese attacked him. Can you believe it? They tried to kill Chester! I'm gonna get Dad's gun when we get home, and I'm gonna come back here and blow 'em all to smithereens!"

"I don't blame you for feeling that way, Trav, but will that help Chester?"

"I don't know," he growled, "but it'll sure help me!" The boy grew silent, watching as his mother dabbed flecks of blood from Chester's neck and breast. "Why'd they do it, Mom?" he suddenly asked. "They're all Canadian geese, ain't . . . aren't they? How come they tried to kill him?"

"I don't know," Lois responded slowly. "Many reasons, most likely. I read somewhere that geese mate for life. Maybe those were already mated and thought Chester was a threat. Seems to me, though, from the cuts he has here where his leg is missing, that they attacked him because he was different, even strange, to them. Chickens do that, and fish, picking at a wound until the wounded one dies. I suppose geese do it, too."

"But why?"

Lois gave Chester one last dab, leaned back, and looked at her son, hoping that she could say what she felt certain he needed to hear. Travis was watching her without expression, waiting, and she knew she would never have a better time. *Help*, she pleaded mentally, prayerfully, and then she began.

"Sometimes, Trav, people are like chickens and fish and geese. They pick at those who are different. Your great-grandfather Hyrum was crippled, and people picked at him most of his life. They even picked at your great-grandmother Ida Mae, after she married him; and my father said that as a child he got a little of it, too. Picking at folks who are different seems to be the bad side of human nature."

"Yeah," Travis said slowly, "I know what you mean. I hate it!"

"Sure you do, Trav, and I don't blame you. But it's still real, and we have to deal with it like Chester does. See? He's not all upset and angry. He's ready to get along with his life. He might be different from those geese out there, but he still likes himself. He's perfectly contented to be who he is. Don't you think that's a pretty good quality or attitude?"

"Yeah, I guess."

"Can *you* be like that, do you think? Can you like yourself even if others think you are different?"

Travis shrugged and looked away. "I dunno," he answered quietly. "Maybe."

"Well, *I* think you can. But, Trav, you have a brother who's being picked apart maybe worse than Chester was. I'm awfully worried about him."

"Who? Jason? He's—"

"Not Jason, Trav. Steve."

"Ha! Nobody's picking Steve apart!"

"Yes, they are."

"Well, it ain . . . isn't me! He's mad at me for some stupid reason or another, and—"

"It isn't you, Trav. It's himself. Steve doesn't like himself very much right now, and because of that he doesn't like anyone else very much, either."

"Boy, that's the truth!"

"Trav, you can help Steve if you want to."

"Oh, sure."

"You can! But you must want to. Do you?"

"I dunno. Not unless he lets up on Chester."

"He will. I promise! You do what I tell you, and it'll work like magic."

Travis looked dubiously at his mother. "How?"

"Trav, Jesus tells us that there are two kinds of greatness, his kind and the world's kind. According to the world's plan, the great are taken care of by others. According to Jesus' plan, the great do the ministering, the taking care of. Jesus used the word *servant*, meaning that they gave service. In other words, the greatest people were those who did the most serving. Now, Trav, I want you to be great to Steve. I want you to minister to him, to serve him."

"Huh? Mom, I don't . . ."

"Don't worry. It won't be hard. All you have to do is act like you like him."

"Well, I do, but . . ."

"See. I told you it would be easy. Now, every day this next week I want you to concentrate on being nice to him. I want you to smile at him, speak to him, listen when he speaks, respond positively to his ideas, and most important, I want you to touch him, to put your hand on his shoulder once in a while."

"Aw, Mom," Travis complained, embarrassed. "I don't want to do that. Besides, he'll probably knock my block off."

Lois grinned. "It's important, Trav. And I promise, he won't hurt you. What you are doing is building Steve's self-esteem. When he realizes that you like him, then he'll start to like himself. After that he'll decide that he likes you and Chester. It's an automatic reflex, sort of."

"How do you know it'll work?"

"I've seen it. I've even done it a few times."

"Like with Mrs. Sudsup?" Travis asked, trying to hide his impish grin.

Lois looked at her son, smiled at his teasing, and then sighed. "She's a hard one, all right. And you haven't helped much, either, you *or* Chester."

"I know, Mom. I'm sorry, too. I didn't know she was gonna be in the bathroom that day."

Lois giggled. "Believe me, she didn't know you would be in there, either. I've never seen two people go so fast in opposite directions. But I'll tell you something else, young man. I'm not giving up on that lady. One way or another she's going to find out we're her friends. You can bet on that! Now, will you give it a try with Steve?"

Travis nodded, and so Lois reached out and hugged him. "Trav," she said gently, "you'll be blessed for this, I know you will. Maybe the Lord will even help you with Chester."

"I hope so," the boy replied quietly. "I really do."

Chapter 14
An Idea Comes to a Brother

It's interesting how people react when they're subjected to a little sincere kindness. Frankly, it's pretty hard for most folks to deal with it (probably because it happens so rarely), and it was certainly that way with Steve.

The day after Lois had spoken with her youngest son, Travis smiled at Steve and said good morning. At first Steve was shocked. Then he grumbled something about "What's wrong with him?" And then for the next little while he stewed about it and cast oblique glances at Travis whenever he could.

Travis, however, paid little attention to the strange behavior of his older brother, except of course to smile at him now and then. Well, poor Steve got more confused than ever, until finally he did what one would normally expect a person in such a situation to do. He became angry.

"What're you grinning at?" he snapped.

"Nothing," Travis replied meekly. "Just you."

"Whaddaya mean by that?"

"Nothing. I was just smiling because I like you."

"Sure," Steve snarled. "Since when?"

"Since always," Travis replied, turning away. "I'm glad I'm your brother."

Well, how does a guy get mad at a statement like that? It can't be done, not if the statement is made to a basically good kid. And Steve was basically good. So he didn't get angry, he just got more confused. By the next day, with Travis still smiling and saying hi and such, Steve could hardly handle it any longer.

"Mom," he asked when he was alone with her, "is Trav all right?"

"I think so," she answered, surprised. "Why?"

"Oh," Steve grumbled, "he's just acting weird."

"Really? What's he doing?"

"Oh, smiling and saying stuff to me and that kind of junk."

Lois smiled. "I see. Well, I don't know *exactly* what is going on, Steve, but I did hear Trav say the other morning that he really likes you."

"Me? Come on. Him and Chester *both* hate me."

"Oh, I don't think so, Steve. That certainly wasn't what he said. By the way, would you get the vacuum cleaner out for me?"

Steve turned away to get the vacuum, and Lois's smile spread from ear to ear. It was working, at least with Steve. It was working very well.

Three days later, after a continuous round of the same "strange" behavior by Travis, which followed continuous encouragement from Lois, and was always followed by the same continuous round of confusion by Steve, the poor kid almost fell over when Travis walked up to him, put his hand on the older boy's shoulder, and spoke.

"Steve," he queried, "I need your help getting Chester to fly."

At first Steve was too shocked to answer. Besides, the pressure of his younger brother's hand on his shoulder was so unusual and so unexpected that he didn't know how to react. And honestly he wanted to say yes, he'd help right then, but there's this little thing called pride, which must be a very important commodity the way some people protect and preserve it.

"Bug off," he snarled, doing his best to make his voice sound mean.

Travis jumped and dropped his hand, and then with sincere sadness on his face he walked away. Well, Steve felt lower than a worm undermining a gopher hole, and he was mentally kicking himself for being such a creep when, incredibly, Travis turned around and smiled.

"Anyway," the boy called, "when you get a chance, come help us. I really need you. We'll be down at the barn."

Well, it took Steve exactly forty-five minutes to make his way across the pasture and down to the old barn. Travis and Jenni were already there, as was Chester, and so Steve didn't exactly walk right up. Rather, he leaned against an apple tree, stuck his hands in his Levi's, watched, and grinned in spite of himself.

And to be truthful, what he was seeing was pretty funny. Trav, as serious as anyone in the whole world, was out in front of Chester giving frantic but totally unheeded flight instructions. At the moment, Travis was flapping his arms up and down, yelling at Chester to pay attention. The bird, however, was with Jenni, leaning against her, and was making no movement at all, especially toward flight.

"Come on," Travis groaned as he walked back toward the goose. "You've got to try, you dumb bird. Here. Like this."

With that Travis reached down, pulled the gander's wings out from his body, and physically flapped them up and down as hard as he could. As you can imagine, though, Chester fought the action and quickly broke free one wing from the boy's grasp. With a loud clicking Chester turned on Travis, making blitzkrieg attacks on the boy's face. Ducking his head and covering his face with his arms, Travis rolled free, and the entire flight instruction program disintegrated into giggling kids and hissing and clicking bird.

Suddenly, however, Chester noticed Steve. Instantly the bird's demeanor changed. Puffing his feathers out, he launched himself straight at the boy. Steve, startled, grabbed for the upper limbs of the tree; and Travis meanwhile pulled the goose to a stop. Then, while Steve watched in fascination, Travis "talked" to the goose, making noises until he gradually calmed down.

"Sorry," Travis said at last. "You can come down now. He won't chase you."

"How do I know that?"

"Just trust me, I guess," Travis replied, smiling.

Slowly Steve climbed down out of the tree, his eyes never leaving the goose.

"What does *he* want?" Jenni asked, making no attempt at hiding the contempt that was in her voice.

"I asked for his help, Jen. We need it."

"How?"

"Yeah," Steve responded. "How?"

Travis stooped and picked up his goose. "I don't know, for sure. I just know that Jenni and I can't do it alone. But you're the fastest runner in the family, Steve, and somehow that ought to help."

"Why doesn't Chester fly by himself?" Jenni suddenly asked.

Travis groaned, flopped onto the ground, pushed Chester away from his ears, and stared at the sky.

"I don't know, Jen."

"You do, too," Steve declared. "You told me. It's because he can't run. They're like an airplane on a runway. Their bodies are too heavy and their wing movements too slow to give them instant lift-off like the smaller birds have."

"Gee, Steve," Travis said, impressed. "How do you know that stuff? I didn't tell you all that."

"I read it in a book at school. You know, it's what Dad calls another tidbit out of my mental encyclopedia of useless trivia."

Jenni giggled. "Yeah, Daddy says you're full of those tidbit things. But, Steve, what's a tidbit?"

Travis and Steve both laughed aloud, Jenni got a hurt look on her face, and Travis suddenly remembered a similar question he had asked not many years before, when he had been laughed at. It was at a family council on honesty, and his father was extolling the virtues of honest people. He began talking about famous ones and finally asked each of the kids if they'd promise to become honest. Steve responded immediately by saying that when he grew up he was going to be like Abe Lincoln.

Their mother jumped on that and asked the other children if they would make the same promise. Each said yes until it got to Travis, and he didn't know what to say because he was so confused.

Finally, after much urging, he said yes, but then almost instantly he asked the question—the one he'd never forget, the one that made his ears burn every time he recalled it.

"But, Mom," he queried innocently, "what's 'a blinkin'?"

Everyone had burst out laughing; he'd felt sillier than a blind bear in a bramble patch, and now he could see how funny it had been. "Jen," he said, grinning, "I didn't mean to make you feel bad, honest. Let me tell you about a dumb question *I* once asked, one that Steve got me into."

He did so; they all laughed; and Chester, bobbing his head up and down, went for Trav's ears again with his beak. After a few minutes of wrestling, Travis pushed his pet away, and then, struggling to his feet, he spoke.

"Well, I guess we'd better get teaching you again, you goofy bird. I just wish you'd—"

"Travis," Steve interrupted suddenly, "I have an idea."

Travis and Jenni stared at the older boy expectantly, both almost afraid to hear what he was about to suggest. "Well?" Travis finally asked, his voice hesitant.

"It might not work," Steve went on, "but then it might, too. Like you said, I'm a pretty fast runner, and I was thinking that maybe if I held Chester so his wings were free and then started running . . ."

"Yeah!" Travis shouted. "That's a *great* idea! Come here, Chester. Steve's going to show you what flying feels like."

Carefully then, Steve took the goose, which protested only a little at what he was suffering. Gingerly Steve held the bird out before him, making certain that the wings were free. Then, slowly, he started to run.

Well, you've never heard such a racket as then commenced. Travis and Jenni were shouting and squealing, Chester was honking, and Steve was hollering for the bird to get his wings and tail out of his eyes. All in all it was a fairly noisy experience. It was also an interesting one, for after a bit Chester stretched his neck out and actually acted a whole lot like he knew what he was doing. When Steve finally stopped running and made his way back, with Chester hopping along beside him, he encountered a pretty ecstatic little brother.

"Steve," he screamed, "did you see him? Did ya? His head was out like it needs to be, and he had his wings out. It was great! It really was. You did it!"

"Let me get my wind," the boy panted, "and I'll do it again, faster. At the end of the run I'll let him go, too, and we'll see what he does. I hope it works, too, 'cause I've got to get to my practice."

Anxiously they waited until Steve's sides quit heaving. Finally he signaled Travis to bring the goose to him. He held Chester out before him and once more began to run. Faster he went, faster and faster, and suddenly Chester's neck was out and his wings were spread.

"Now!" Travis yelled. "Now! Push him out!"

Steve did, and slid to a stop as Chester glided beyond his fingers, appearing to fly.

Well, Travis was whooping for joy; Jennie was screaming; and Steve was about to do the same when Chester's wings suddenly folded and the poor goose slammed into the ground and skidded ignominiously forward.

Quickly Steve ran up and gathered the dusty bird into his arms. He was standing, holding it that way, when Travis and Jenni arrived.

"Is he okay?" Travis asked fearfully.

"Yeah, I think so."

For a moment there was silence, and then Travis spoke again, his voice trembling with excitement. "Boy, did you see that? He almost flew!"

"Almost only counts in horseshoes, Trav."

"Yeah, but, Steve, he's learning! I can tell it! That's the best he ever did."

Steve grinned. "Good," he said. "We'll do it again tonight. Here, Trav. Take him. I've got to get."

Carefully Travis took the goose from his brother, who turned and started back across the pasture.

"Steve," Travis suddenly called out. "Thanks. You really helped."

Steve turned around and looked at his younger brother, and suddenly he broke into a real grin. "So did you," he answered. "So did you. I'm glad I'm your brother, too."

SEPTEMBER

Chapter 15
A Little More of the Legend

How time flies when you're having fun. Or, to say it another way, how time flies when a deadline is coming. And that kind of time flying is a whole lot worse to deal with. Travis learned that principle the hard way; for suddenly summer was over and he was in school again and the rope climb was back before him and he was no more ready than he had been in the spring. And even worse, Thanksgiving was coming, and Chester still couldn't fly. Needless to say, the boy was pretty discouraged, and everyone in the family knew it.

"Hank," Lois asked late one night, "have you explained that competition-opposition thing to Travis so that he understands it?"

"Why? Is he having problems again?"

"I don't know," Lois responded. "He's surely discouraged, though. I assume that trouble is coming, even if it hasn't happened yet. School competition isn't going to go away, you know."

Hank grinned. "Good old practical Lois," he said softly. "You know how to get right to the core, don't you? Yes, I've talked to him several times. No, I don't think he understands what I'm saying. However, I think *I'm* beginning to."

"You mean understand?"

"Yes. I keep remembering things, and it's starting to make more sense."

"What do you remember?"

"Well, you know what I told you about Harold's legend of the Pale God and what he taught? The other day I remembered something else that Harold told me. Apparently the Pale God taught the people a game or contest or something where the winners were those who helped the opposing team to score the most points. For the life of me I can't comprehend how such a game could be played, but Harold told me that there are still Indian customs today that show vestiges of it.

"In the Northwest some tribes hold a potlatch where they give away to other people everything that they have. The Plains tribes call the same thing simply a giveaway. They do it to express both joy and sorrow, for it either shows tremendous gratitude or it earns the right to tremendous spiritual comfort. The thought behind it, however, seems to be selflessness."

"And you think that's the key?"

"Well, at least it's the ultimate goal. First, though, a person needs to be satisfied with himself. Then

145

he can start concentrating on others instead of old number one."

"Which brings us back to Travis and competition," Lois concluded, smiling slightly.

"Yes, it does," Hank agreed. "Somehow I need to show him that success is doing better than himself, not better than someone else. If I can find a way to teach him to integrate that idea into his life, then athletic events and other kinds of contests will stop being threatening to him and will become more enjoyable. Now, pray for me, will you? To teach him that, I'm going to need all the help I can get."

Smiling, Lois put her arms around her husband's neck, kissed him, and told him softly that she loved him. A little later, together, they prayed that Hank would receive the help he so badly needed.

Chapter 16
The Ball Game

One day, about two weeks after Hank and Lois's late-night conversation, Hank had an idea that he thought might work. He'd sent the boys out to the barn to work with Travis on The Rope, hoping that some progress might be achieved. Jason and Steve had rolled their eyes in disgust, Travis had groaned aloud, but they had gone, anyway, because their dad had spoken.

A little while later, after Travis had failed twice and Steve had climbed The Rope easily, Hank walked through the door. After watching Travis give The Rope his best shot, which was still nowhere near good enough, Hank praised his son for his improvement and then gently reminded him that he wasn't in competition with anyone but himself.

"Yeah," Travis groaned again, "but I'm lousy

competition for me. I ain't . . . I'm not ever going to climb that stupid thing!"

"Hey, don't be discouraged. You're making progress."

"Sure! Dad, there's ten or twelve feet of that rope I've never even touched yet. I'm just not athletic. I can't *do* those kinds of things."

"Trav, Mr. Larson doesn't think Chester will ever fly, either. Do you agree with him?"

"Heck, no! I'm gonna teach . . ."

Hank raised his hand and stopped his son, and then he grinned. "You tell me you're never going to climb a rope, but I don't believe that any more than you don't believe what Mr. Larson says about Chester. You're every bit as courageous as your goose, and you have just as much stick-to-itiveness. Trav, I *know* you're going to climb that rope!"

In the silence that followed, Chester hopped to The Rope, took some strands in his bill, and began twisting his head back and forth, pulling The Rope back toward Travis. Everyone burst out laughing, and Travis, after a little prodding and coaching from Hank, gave The Rope another try. But it was no good. No matter what he did or how hard he tried, he could not get beyond his previous high mark.

"See!" he said, his eyes filling with tears. "I *can't* do it. I just can't."

Gently Hank reached over and tousled the boy's hair. "You'll do it," he replied gently. "Maybe not today, or even tomorrow, but you'll do it! You're a winner if I ever saw one."

148

"Dad?" Jason suddenly asked. "Trav says you told him that winning was evil."

"Yeah, Dad," Steve added, "Jase and I are both on teams, and I don't think that's being evil. In fact, I like it, 'cause we've got a great team. Besides, what's so wrong with wanting to win?"

Hank stood for a moment, looking thoughtfully at each of his sons. Finally, sitting down on an old bale of hay, he spoke.

"Winning isn't evil, boys. I never did say that. In fact, being a winner is vital to happiness. No, what I told Travis was that some things about competition seem to be evil. At least that's what a friend of mine once told me."

"Do you believe him?"

"Yes, I think I do."

"But, Dad, sports are great, and they help us a lot. Besides, you can't get rid of all of them! A part of our economy is based on them."

Hank grinned. "No, Jase, I couldn't do away with sports. Nor would I want to, at least not right now. What I would like to get rid of, though, are some of the negative results of competition."

"Like what?"

"Well, did I ever tell you about our state championship basketball teams?"

"Yeah," Jason grinned. "About a thousand times."

Hank laughed. "I thought I might have. Well, sit down here and let me tell you something else that I don't think I've ever talked about."

Sensing one of their father's stories coming up, the boys relaxed into the hay to listen. Travis even

149

managed to click Chester into silence, and that took some serious clicking.

"You know," Hank began, "that I was on two state championship teams. Those were my sophomore and junior years. But the year I really won was the year I was a senior. That's the year I played my best ball, and that's the year I want to tell you about.

"That year we had the best team you've ever seen. I was the weakest starter, and frankly, I was pretty darn good."

All the boys groaned; Hank grinned because he knew they were listening, and then he continued. "We won our regional championship easily, and so when we went to state we drew a bye the first round. Because we didn't have anything else to do, and because our coach wanted us to know our competition, we spent that first day watching the other teams play.

"Now, I'll have to admit that I don't recall anything significant about those other teams. They were all above average, except of course for one. That was a Cinderella team, a bunch of hayseeds from some tiny little high school way down in the south end of the state. As I recall, there wasn't really a standout player on their team. Nor did they have anyone of great height. On the other hand, I've never in my life seen a bunch of guys who played with such intensity and such unity.

"Five minutes into their first game and I was cheering for them. And I wasn't alone, either. Every kid on my team felt the same. We really wanted them to win. And against all the odds, they did.

150

"Well, for an entire week we watched those guys, and every game they played we cheered them on. In fact, pretty soon it seemed like we were all old friends. We knew all their last names, they knew ours, and we horsed around together off the court. For that week we were all buddies.

"Incredible as it sounds, those guys won every game. The scores were close, but they still won. And, as you might have guessed, so did we. So, for the championship game, we ended up facing each other."

Hank paused and looked at each of his boys, grinning at their look of anticipation. It was great fun, he felt, telling stories to his sons. It was one of the surest ways he had of still being a hero.

"Well," he said, continuing, "that championship game was quite a contest. We had more talent than they did, and we had greater skills. The thing was, those guys wanted to win. But so did we, believe me. We'd talked to each other about it all week, and we were psyched up as high as we could have been.

"During the game the lead changed sides continually, back and forth, back and forth, until finally, with thirteen seconds to go, we had forged ahead on a couple of free throws I made, and led by five. I was a hero, and I don't mind saying, modestly, of course, that I was in rare form. I had played the best game of my life, and so had my teammates. All of us figured we had the game sewn up.

"But then one of their guards, a freckle-faced kid with glasses who hadn't done much all night but handle the ball, brought it down again and fired off a long jump shot. He missed, but in my eager-ness to rebound I fouled him, and so he went to the line to shoot two.

"He shot; his first attempt hit nothing but the bottom of the net; and I wondered where he'd been all night. They were still down by four, though, and mentally we were already celebrating."

"Dad," Jason interrupted, "is this for real?"

"Jase, have I ever lied to you?"

"Uh . . . yeah. A few times. I mean, you kid around a lot . . . I mean . . ."

Hank laughed. "Jase, get out your Bible and I'll swear on it. I promise this is the truth, the whole truth, and nothing but the truth. Good enough?"

Jason nodded, and Hank saw with satisfaction that Steve and Travis were nodding as well. He had them, all right.

"Anyway, boys, that little guard with the thick glasses set for his second free throw. He took a long time with it, and then do you know what he did? He didn't shoot, at least not for the net. In-stead he shot the ball hard against the front rim, stepped forward, jumped into the air, and took his own intentional rebound. Leaping again, he climbed about a hundred yards into the sky, hung there forever, and let go with a soft little five-foot jumper.

"Swish! Twelve seconds to go and our lead was cut to two."

Hank paused, picked up a strand of hay, and taking his time he began splitting it in half.

"What happened next?" Steve finally asked, his teenage impatience getting the best of him.

"Oh, not much." Hank grinned, sitting up as if

to leave. "You guys look tired. I don't think you want to hear the rest of it."

"Daaaaad," they wailed in unison.

Hank's grin grew even wider, and tossing the hay aside he leaned back.

"Okay. It was our ball with twelve seconds to go. The other guard on our team passed the ball into me, and I was just turning down the court when that same freckled-faced guard came in from nowhere and somehow took the ball away from me. He didn't do much with it, either. He just flew into the air right where he was and let fly with a three-hundred-foot jumper that went about a mile into the air, came down, and again hit nothing but the bottom of the net. The game then went into overtime, and they won 79–75."

"Is that all?" Steve asked, sounding disappointed.

"Almost, Steve. What happened next is what I want each of you to remember. When they won, I started crying."

"Boy," Jason responded, "I don't blame you!"

"No, Jase, you don't understand, and that's what I meant about the problem of competition. You see, you think my team and I lost, and we didn't."

"You did, too! You just said so."

"No, I said the other team won."

"But that's the same thing."

"No, it isn't, Steve, though in a competitive sense you'd be right. Listen carefully, now, and I'll try to explain the difference.

"It wasn't because we'd lost that I cried. It was because *they'd* won. I was actually so thrilled by their happiness and excitement that I started crying.

153

I'd never done that before, wept for joy because of another person's success, and it was a new and confusing feeling for me."

"How did the other guys on your team handle it?"

"All but one felt about like I did. That one kid was bitter, and for all I know he still is. But he isn't the important one in this story. The rest of us are the ones I want you to remember. We were the ones who were suddenly rejoicing in the success of others.

"Those hayseed kids were not competition to us, they were opposition. And we were opposition to them as well. Because of that, there were no losers in that game. We were all winners, because we'd all played the best game of our lives, and because we came off that court, every one of us, a better man."

"Except for one," Travis said quietly.

"That's right, Trav. Except for one. And if he hasn't changed, he's still losing."

"But why?"

"Because unless he's changed, he still thinks there have to be losers as well as winners in sports, and for that matter in every game we play in life."

"But he's right, Dad. Somebody has to lose!"

"According to a score, maybe. But remember, scores are for coaches and fans. I'm talking about higher things than that. I'm talking about the heart of a *true* man or woman, a true athlete. That's where the real winning goes on.

"Boys, I'm convinced that when a person can rejoice in another person's strengths and successes, even when those strengths and successes aren't his own, then that person is a real winner. That's what winning means.

"Too often our sense of competition does not allow us to feel that way. We become so caught up in wanting victory, in wanting the opposite team or person to lose, that we forget about the real spirit of winning. That spirit rejoices in great accomplishment no matter whose it is, and it accepts with gratitude the need for self-improvement which another's success shows. Competition doesn't let us feel that way very often, and that's probably why my friend Harold said it was evil."

For a moment there was silence, the only sounds being the soft clickings of Chester, who by now was digging with his beak into the hay.

"Does that mean," Travis asked quietly, breaking the silence of the late afternoon, "that I ought to be thankful for Coach because he's made me want so badly to climb The Rope?"

Both Jason and Steve started to snicker, but with a wave of his hand Hank stopped them.

"Trav," he said gently, "I can't tell you how impressed I am that you said that. I really think you understand. Harold Gos-Coyote told me that we should give thanks for all opposition, for we should appreciate the strength it gives us. When we did that, he said, then we would be true men. I do believe, Travis, that you're growing up."

Travis's heart swelled with pride, and he was just wondering what to say next when from the driveway up near their house an automobile horn sounded. Scrambling from the barn, Hank and his sons immediately recognized old Mr. Larson's new pickup; and they all hurried across the pasture to greet him.

Chapter 17
Travis's Bargain

"Well, arid land-o'-Goshen," the old man growled as Hank and his sons hurried toward him. "What in tarnation you folks doin' down at the old barn?"

"Just learning a little championship ball," Hank replied, catching his breath. "Did you come for your sheep?"

"Nope, not yet. By the way, did you lose any?"

"No, sir," Jason responded quickly, "we ain't lost a one."

"Haven't," Hank corrected.

"Yeah," Jason said, embarrassed that he'd needed correction in front of the old man, "haven't."

For a moment Mr. Larson stared at Jason, taking the young man in from head to foot.

"You know," the old man growled, "you're going to be taller'n me yet, Jase, if you keep on growin'."

Jason looked down at the old man and grinned.

"You, too, Steve," the old man added. "I can't

believe how you boys are growing. Now, where's that runt of a Travis?"

"Behind you," the boy replied quickly.

Mr. Larson turned and then stepped back, startled.

"Whoa," he shouted in surprise. "What in blue blazes have you got there?"

"Chester," the boy responded proudly. "He's growed some, ain't he?"

"Grown some, hasn't he," Hank corrected quietly, wondering as he did if his sons were ever going to learn to speak correctly.

Travis ducked his head, as embarrassed as his older brother had been.

"I should smile and say he has," the old man went on excitedly, paying no attention to Hank. "Put him down and let's take a good look at him."

Quickly Travis lowered the almost full-grown goose to the ground. For a moment Chester stood still. Then with a slight clicking noise he turned and hopped away.

"Mmmmm," Mr. Larson grumbled, "ain't he a beaut!"

"Isn't," Travis corrected instantly without really thinking about what he was saying.

"Whaddaya mean isn't?" the old man snarled. "It's ain't. Only it ain't ain't, 'cause he is. He's a beaut, just like I said. My oh my, oh my, oh my. Won't me and the old woman feast come this Thanksgiving."

"But . . . but, Mr. Larson," Travis said in a whisper, "I . . ."

"Well, what is it, boy? Speak up. What's on your mind?"

Travis took a deep breath and looked up at the awesome old man. "You . . . you can't eat Chester, sir. You just can't."

"Why not, lad? He's my goose, ain't he?"

"Well, yes . . . but . . ."

"Then the matter's settled!"

For a moment Travis dropped his gaze, his heart aching with the agony of what Mr. Larson had said. But then, as Travis started to turn away, he noticed Chester eyeing Gerty, obviously giving thought to chasing the huge old cow across the pasture. The thought of his little goose chasing a monster cow suddenly filled Travis with a courageous wrath of his own, and without even considering what might come of what he was about to do, he spun around on the old man.

"No, it ain't . . . isn't settled!" Travis shouted angrily, shocking everyone there, but most especially his father, who quickly turned an uncomfortable shade of red.

"You caught him, all right," the boy continued, plunging ahead, "and you paid me to raise him, too. But that don't change nothing . . . anything. Chester's still a wild free goose. He can't fly yet, because he hasn't been big enough for long enough to learn. But I'm giving you fair warning, Mr. Larson. One leg or not, I'm going to teach him to fly! Then come Thanksgiving he'll be long gone and you and your wife will have to find something else to eat! And you can have your old money back, too!"

For a long moment the old man stared down at the trembling boy, obviously amazed. "Well, arid

159

land-o'-Goshen," he finally growled, "this boy of yours has sand, Hank, and no matter his sawed-off size. You'd ought to be proud of him. Why, I ain't been stood up to like that since the old woman come down with the rheumatiz.

"Trav, I admire your spunk, and because of that, you got yourself a deal. That Chester-goose flies off south under his own power before the last Tuesday in November and the whole thing's canceled. You don't have to pay the money back, either.

"Howsomever, if that critter's still around come Thanksgiving, which I'm fair-to-middlin' certain he's going to be, then the deal's still on and there won't be no complaints from you. Fair enough?"

Travis, a surge of hope lifting his heart, nodded, and so the old man went on. "Now, listen up, son. It's like I tell you every year with them bummer lambs. You can't go buildin' no fond attachments for a critter what's meant for the pot. What comes from that is gettin' hurt. Every time! And mark my words, hurt is what you'll be come November. I guarantee it."

"He'll be all right, Mr. Larson," Hank quickly interjected. "It's just that Chester has done some interesting and even fine things for our family, and it's hard not to get attached. But don't worry. If he's still here come Thanksgiving, he'll be yours.

"Now, why don't you come around behind the house with me? We're having a problem with the roof, and I want to make you an offer."

Mr. Larson groaned. "Merciful heavens," he grumbled. "I don't know if I can afford too many more of your offers, Hank. Somehow, between you and

Trav, I seem to be coming up on the short end of every stick I take up. But come on. Let's go look. I'm at least willing to listen."

Together then the two men moved away, and Travis stood staring after them.

"Don't worry, Trav," Jason said quietly as he put his arm around his younger brother's shoulders. "We'll think of something, just wait and see."

Chapter 18
Jenni and Her Faith Again

A few days later Travis came home from school with a face longer than a stretched-out boa constrictor.

"Hi, Trav," Lois called as he slammed through the door. There was no answer, and so she turned around to see what was going wrong in the life of her son.

"Problems?" she asked quietly.

"That's the understatement of the year," he growled.

"Can I help?"

"Yeah. Hire somebody to assassinate Coach."

"Now, Trav, you know better than to talk like that."

Slowly the boy looked up at his mother. "Yeah, I know better. I just wish somebody'd taught *him*. He'd have to graduate from three colleges just to become human."

"What's he done?" Lois asked quickly so that she could hide her smile.

"Ah, nothing much. It's just that stupid rope climb again. What is it with him and that rope, anyway?"

"Is there going to be another contest?"

Slowly Travis nodded.

"And you don't want to be laughed at again."

"Would you?" the boy snarled.

"No, I wouldn't. But I'd sure do something else about it than sit around getting angry."

"Like what? Practice?"

"Obviously."

"Aw, Mom."

"Well, Trav, you've given up again, and that isn't like you."

"Yeah, but if you knew how bad I was . . ."

"Have you given up on Chester flying?"

"What? Course I haven't. He's getting better, and . . ."

"And so are you, young man. Nor have your father and I given up on you. Not even a little bit have we given up. I know you're going to climb that rope, but you can't do it unless you practice. Why don't you go down to the barn and do a little climbing before supper?"

"I'll go with you," Jenni shouted.

"Jenni," Lois scolded, "pipe down, for goodness' sake. Yelling like that will wake the dead."

Jenni giggled, Travis smiled, and together they left the house, set Chester free of his pen, and crossed the orchard to the old barn.

For a while Travis again tried to climb The Rope.

He really tried. But no matter how hard he gritted his teeth and strained, and no matter how high he jumped to start, it did no earthly good. He just couldn't get any higher than about twelve feet. Over and over he tried, while Jennie cheered and Chester honked and flapped about. But it was no use. Travis simply could not climb that rope.

"Doggonnit," he muttered disgustedly as he and his little sister slowly made their way back through the twilight toward their home. "Chester and I are a real pair, ain't we?"

"Aren't we, Trav."

"Yeah, I mean aren't we. He can't fly for sour apples, and I can't climb that stupid rope. We're sure a team. But, Jenn, I'm more worried about Chester than I am about me. If he's going to escape Thanksgiving, he's *got* to learn to fly. I tell you, it's his only chance. I mean after all, he's a bird, isn't he? You'd think he could learn."

"Trav," Jenni asked suddenly, "can every bird fly?"

"Well, no, I guess not. There's ostriches and—"

"Then how come Chester should?" Jenni asked, interrupting her brother. "Remember the other night when you didn't want to go play ball?"

"Yeah, I remember. So what?"

"Well, you said not all boys were supposed to be alike. You said not everybody was supposed to like the same things. Didn't you say that?"

"Uh-huh."

"Well, isn't it the same with gooses? If all boys aren't supposed to be all alike, why should Chester be the same as other gooses?"

164

Travis, dumbfounded, stared in disbelief at his seven-year-old sister. How in the world, he wondered, had she ever thought of that? She was right, of course, in a funny sort of way. But sometimes the things she said scared him to death. Sometimes Jenni just didn't sound like she was seven.

"Uh, I guess you're right," he replied lamely. "Only, how are we ever going to get Chester to leave before Thanksgiving if he won't fly?"

"I don't know, Trav. Maybe he'll get away somehow else. But Mommy and Daddy both say that if we pray, God will help us. I bless you and Chester every night. You'll think of something. I know you will. I've borrowed you *all* my faith."

Travis looked at Jenni and mentally scratched his head again. That little girl was really something. She was either really smart or really dumb, and she sure didn't act dumb. Faith, he thought then. Maybe that's all it was. She just had tons of faith. He knew that he didn't have that much, but maybe, if he had faith in her faith . . .

A couple of hours later, just as he was crawling into bed, Jenni's prayers were answered, and Travis had his idea. Quickly he enlisted the enthusiastic support of Jason and Jenni and a converted Steve, and after he had thoroughly checked out several of his father's telephone directories, he crawled into bed and had no trouble going to sleep—no trouble at all.

165

Chapter 19
Some Are Caught, One Is Not

"I'm telling you, Lois, I'm worried about that boy."

The warm fall sun, coming through the kitchen window, was striking the table at which Hank Tilby was sitting. Idly he watched the dust particles dancing in the rays of light, dust particles fluffed into the air as his wife, Lois, vigorously cleaned her cupboards. She was really something, he thought. No matter what else happened, she was always busy. And no matter what kind of a budget he put her on, their home was always neat and clean. Yes, sir, Hank knew he'd been far more than lucky when he married her.

"What do you think he'll do, honey?" she asked, concerned.

"Oh, it isn't what he'll do. There's nothing that he can do. It's what he'll go through when it finally happens. If Travis can't get Chester to fly, I'm afraid it's going to be pretty rough on him."

"Oh, Hank, what are we going to do?"

"I guess we'd better talk with him, try to prepare him. Other than helping with Chester, I don't know what else we can do."

Hank stood then and walked to where his wife was working. Putting his arms around her, he spoke gently.

"You know, Lois, Trav's only problem is that he loves Chester. And how can we fault him for that? I love you, and I'd feel pretty bad if someone told me they were going to stuff you and eat you for Thanksgiving dinner."

"I *hope* so." Lois smiled, snuggling up to her husband.

"I'm serious, honey. I'd guess it's about the same thing to Travis. I remember a dog I had once, old Caesar, that I loved with all my heart and soul. I'm sure Travis feels the same way about Chester."

"He does, Hank. I know that, too. But what really frightens me is the feeling I have that Chester somehow loves Travis."

"I think he does as well, but why is that bad?"

"Hank, if Chester has emotionally mated with Travis, so to speak, then even if he does fly it won't matter. The goose will never leave here."

Hank's face showed his surprise. "I see what you mean," he said slowly. "Mr. Larson will have him for Thanksgiving dinner no matter what Travis does."

"That's right."

"Well, what should we do?"

"I've thought about calling Mr. Larson and explaining things to him. He's such a good man that I'm sure he'd understand. Do you think we should?"

Hank stood, walked to the window, and looked out. The morning was beautiful, and everything seemed so peaceful. The sunlight was gilding the fall-colored leaves on the trees, and the light touch of frost, melted now beneath the early morning warmth, caused the lawn to glisten like a million diamonds. Down in the corral Gerty was contentedly chewing her cud, patiently manufacturing new milk for the family, and the horses were kicking their heels up down in the pasture.

"Trav needs to move Chester's pen," he said quietly. "The goose needs more grass."

"Hank, should we call Mr. Larson?"

Slowly the man turned around and faced his wife. "I almost hate myself for saying this, Lois, but I don't think so. Mr. Larson talked with me about it the other day, and he'll do whatever we want him to do. In my opinion, however, this issue of Chester is one of the hard realities of life that we all encounter from time to time. Travis is going to run into them from now until the day he dies, and the sooner he learns how to deal with them, the better off he'll be."

"But, Hank, he's so young!"

"Well, yes, he is, in a way. But he's also pretty old. Two, three years from now and he'll be working for wages, selling his time to someone else, facing responsibility every day of his life. He's got to know how to do it, and this thing with Chester seems like a pretty major step in that direction."

Lois turned back to the sink, her heart heavy with the certainty that what her husband was saying was right. "How will you tell him?" she asked quietly.

"I don't think we should tell him, Lois. In fact, we may not need to. After all, there's always the chance that we're wrong. Maybe Chester *will* fly, and if he does, maybe he'll leave. Trav is pretty ingenious, and he certainly is working on it."

"But when it comes right down to Thanksgiving, Hank," she asked, turning back to him, "then what do we do?"

"I don't know, honey. I guess we all suffer together. Of course if that time comes and Chester hasn't gone, then we've got to be firm; but we also must be very, very gentle. Our son's heart is involved, and it's at a pretty tender stage right now."

For a moment Lois looked up into her husband's eyes, and then she melted against him.

"You know," she whispered, kissing his ear as she spoke, "I think the Good Lord blessed me with a pretty fine husband. My heart's involved with you, too. And it's *awfully* tender, exactly like the man I love. I'm so glad you're the father of my children."

"Ummmmmmm," Hank mumbled as he nuzzled his wife's neck, "so am I."

Hank and Lois were standing that way, holding each other closely, when Jason bounced into the room, obviously anxious to be on his way to school.

"Ah-ha!" he said, grinning sheepishly. "Caught ya!"

"Eat your heart out," Hank replied, smiling back

at his son. "Someday, though, if you're lucky, you'll get a wife as cute as mine. Then you can do this, too. Now, pay attention and I'll teach you something else."

And then, grabbing his already blushing wife even more securely, Hank bent her over backward and kissed her tenderly on the lips.

"Big deal!" Jason grunted, grinning widely. "What makes you think I don't do that already, with Sheryl?"

"Jason," Lois gasped, twisting away from her husband. "You hadn't better . . ."

"Wow," the boy snickered, "you ought to see us when I walk her home. Wheweee!"

"Jason, if I had any idea you were being serious . . ."

Jason leaned against the refrigerator, grinning. "You know, you're just the opposite of her girlfriends. They're always pushing me to do something, twisting the screws like you wouldn't believe. They even wait for me after school. I told 'em last night to quit bugging me."

"Well, you hadn't better be doing anything, young man! You're too young to start kissing . . ."

"Aw, relax, Mom," the boy said as he dished up a bowl of hot mush from the stove. "I'm too big of a chicken for that kind of stuff. I held her hand once, and that was enough to throw me into a full molt. Maybe when I'm thirty-two or something . . ."

"I'll remember that," Hank said, grinning, "and I'll hold you to it. No kissing until you're thirty-two. By the way, where's your little brother?"

"Which one?"

"Travis."

"Uh . . . I saw him through the window a few minutes ago. He went down to the barn."

"Okay. Thanks, Jase."

Moments later, while Hank and Lois were still talking, Steve walked in.

"Steve," Lois asked, "would you go down to the old barn and get Travis? He's going to be late for school."

"Oh," Steve answered quickly, "he's not there, Mom. He's upstairs asleep. He doesn't look very good, and I don't think he should be disturbed."

"But Jason just . . ."

And then Lois was interrupted as Jenni burst into the kitchen.

"Hi, Mommy and Daddy," she said brightly. "Travis is out teaching Chester to fly, and he probably won't be back before school . . . or maybe even supper."

"Wait just a minute," Hank growled, looking at his wife as he spoke. "Something funny's going on around this place, and I'm going to find out what. Steve, go and get Jase."

Steve, looking suddenly very ill, walked to the door and called his older brother back into the house.

"All right, you three," Hank said sternly, placing his hands upon his hips. "We've talked to three children in the last five minutes about where Travis is, and all three of you have given us a different answer. I think that's called lying, which is something Tilbys do not do. Ever! Now, where is he?"

171

Jason and Steve squirmed uneasily, and Jenni immediately started to cry.

"Jenni, darling," Lois said softly, "we're not angry with you children. We love you. We just don't like dishonesty, do we?"

Slowly Jenni shook her head back and forth. "Uh-uh," she said quickly. "Trav told me about 'a blinkin,' and I want to be that way, too, whatever it is."

Confused, Hank and Lois looked at each other in silence. But then Steve reminded them, the laughter came again, the tension disappeared, and Lois turned once more to her sweet little daughter.

"Now, Jenni," she continued gently, "would you like to tell your daddy and me where Trav is?"

The small girl dried her eyes and looked up. "I don't know, Mommy. He told us last night he'd thought of a way to save Chester, but he didn't want us to tell you where he'd gone until he got back tonight."

"*Tonight?* Is that right?" Hank asked, turning to his oldest son.

"Yes, sir," the boy responded. "He wouldn't tell us no more than that, either."

"*Any* more," Lois corrected absently.

"Yeah, Mom," Jason replied, a tiny smile breaking across his face. "Anyway, he said that if you found out he was gone, we should tell you not to worry. He had Chester with him, so he said he'd be okay."

"Oh, brother!" Hank replied, rolling his eyes in disbelief. "Travis alone, Chester protecting him,

172

and we're not supposed to worry? Lois, I'm going after him."

"I'd say yes, but where would you go?"

"Well, that's a good point. And none of you kids know where he was going?"

The children, their faces honestly blank, shook their heads.

"Okay," Hank said with a sigh, "that's that. But if I had some kind of idea about what he had in his mind . . ."

Well, needless to say, both Hank and Lois waited. They also worried—all day long. But then, who could blame them? Why, a desperate boy and a crippled goose turned loose upon the world is enough to make anybody worry, anybody at all.

Chapter 20
The Cop and the Doc

For an hour Travis walked along the highway, his thumb out whenever a car passed. And although he was hopeful, no one stopped to give him a ride. It may have been because he was so small that no one took his efforts seriously. Or it may have been because of the large goose hopping along beside him. Whichever, after an hour he was totally discouraged and still walking, though very, very slowly.

Of course if he'd had his druthers, he'd rather have left Chester at home, knowing that the goose could be a real drawback to his success. His problem, though, had been in measuring. He simply didn't know how to do it. That's why Chester was with him.

That morning he'd also used Chester as his alarm. He'd discovered months before that Chester always awoke at a specific and fairly early hour. So he'd added two and two and come up with an alarm clock. Interestingly it had never failed to work.

By tying a thread to Chester's leg, draping it up over the light fixture, wrapping it down and around the door handle, stringing it back up and over the shelf bracket, dropping it to the top of his head-board, and then wrapping it around a book which was precariously balanced there, Travis had an ideal (if somewhat risky) alarm. When Chester awakened and stretched, the string was instantly pulled tight. That dislodged the book, which crashed down upon Trav's head and did a fairly good job (as you can imagine) of waking him up. Of course he also got a black eye once, but that was a minor price to pay for such a wonderful Chester-clock.

Anyway, Travis had spirited Chester into his room the night before, rigged his clock, and awakened with only a slight bump on the noggin, just about exactly when he'd planned on awakening. He dressed in the darkness, gulped down a glass of milk, grabbed a couple of slices of bread for him-self and the goose, and crept from the house.

Travis had known that his parents would try to stop him if they caught him, and so he had been extra quiet. Of course Chester didn't know the meaning of the word *quiet*, and the dumb goose had given the boy a couple of bad moments. He'd finally made it, though, had gotten to the highway in good time, and was now discovering how diffi-cult it was to thumb down a ride. He'd asked his brothers and sister to cover for him as long as they could, but it had been over an hour since he'd left, and he could still see where his home was. If his folks missed him now, he knew, they could easily catch him. Travis worried about that a whole lot.

Another car roared past, ignoring him, and then moments later another. Neither stopped, and Travis was feeling terribly alone and discouraged.

"Scrud," he grumbled as he trudged along kicking rocks ahead of him, "why isn't anything ever easy?"

Suddenly Travis heard another car coming up behind him, and halfheartedly he put out his thumb. At that same instant, however, Chester saw something in the bushes and took off after it, ignoring the commands of his young master.

Without even looking at the approaching car, Travis started running and hollering after Chester, pleading for the goose to return before he got into trouble. And then, much to Travis's surprise, he heard the car begin to slow down. Frantically he ran up the road shouting at the errant goose, not even looking to see who was slowing behind him.

Gradually the car pulled up, creeping along in order to keep pace with the running and yelling boy, and still Travis did not look around, for his eyes were busy searching for his feathered pet.

"Hey, kid!" a man's voice called out, "you want a ride or a race?"

Turning for the first time to see who had stopped, Travis almost had a coronary. The car, with its front door swinging open toward him, carried the insignia of the Highway Patrol, and the man inside had a uniform on and carried a gun on his hip that looked more like a cannon than a pistol.

"Uh . . ." Travis gulped. "Uh . . . uh . . ."

"Well, you want a ride or not?"

Travis gulped again and moved slowly toward the car, still without Chester.

"Hurry up, son," the patrolman demanded. "I've got lots to do, so put a cork in the door and let's get moving!"

"Uh . . ." Travis hesitated. "Er . . . okay. But wait just a sec, please. I've got to get Chester."

There was an instant change on the patrolman's face. His smile vanished, his eyes grew cold and calculating, and when he spoke, his voice was steel-hard and filled with menace.

"Kid," he said quietly, "I offered *you* a ride, not all your buddies. If you, and only you, want a ride, then get in! If not, beat it, before I run you in for sluffing school. Whichever, make up your mind. Fast."

Well, the vehicle was rolling again, and Travis *had* to have a ride, so he grabbed the door, shouted for Chester one last time, and started to climb in.

Now, one thing which Travis was always forgetting about Chester was how sudden the goose could be. Mrs. Sudsup, of course, could have testified to that. And at that moment, for some unexplained reason, Chester chose to become sudden once again, giving the patrolman a chance to testify as well.

Travis wasn't even all the way into the patrol car when the big bird exploded out of the bushes. With a wild honking and scrambling he pushed past the boy's legs, hopped and flapped onto the seat of the car, and met that patrolman eyeball to eyeball.

Travis was never certain what it was the officer said then, but it bore no resemblance at all to modern English. Still, it was loud enough, and it was punctuated with such a wild gyrating of the patrolman's body that Chester apparently thought he was under attack. Naturally the poor goose went berserk, and it doesn't take much imagination to guess what happened next.

First, the car left the road altogether and plowed a wildly bumping course along the barrow pit. Second, Chester and the officer went at it hand and bill, feather and skin, in the craziest wrestling match Travis had ever seen. And third, Travis simply closed his eyes, prayed, and did his best to hang on. From then on it was one very interesting ride.

Finally, after what seemed forever, the car hit a small ditch and Travis's head slammed hard into the roof of the vehicle. That did it. Suddenly the whole world was out of control, and things that had been bad before were now worse than awful. Travis, a little loony, thought he was flying, and he was about to raise his arms in acceptance of all the applause when he realized that the cheering he could hear was not cheering at all but screaming, the terrified cries of a wild animal in trouble.

Fearfully he opened his eyes, and then he knew he was in hot water for sure. Chester had the patrolman by the ear; the poor man was yelling and trying to break free and drive the car and stop it all at once; and he was still working on that new language he had invented.

Strangely the officer was doing a fairly creditable job of everything, too. In spite of Chester's opposition, which was somewhat considerable, the man was still putting up a pretty good fight, and he seemed to be growing stronger by the minute.

Eventually, however, he managed to break free and to get his car back onto the road and stopped, which was no mean feat under those conditions. And then he looked at Travis.

For a moment no one moved, and Travis noticed how red the officer's face was becoming. Suddenly the man's fists clenched, his eyes started to bulge, his head started to shake back and forth, and his mouth started saying words that had no sounds to them.

Travis, seeing that, realized that if he didn't think of something fast, he and Chester would be spending the rest of their natural lives dirtying and mopping up floors in the county jail. So, drawing a deep breath and praying with all of his heart that Chester would for once remember something good, Travis made formal introductions.

"Uh . . . Officer, this is my pet goose Chester. Chester, this is a nice policeman. Shake hands with him, okay?"

Now, it's important to understand that Travis had been trying to teach Chester to shake hands (or foot, if you will) for weeks. Trouble was, the goose had never done it. He had come close once with Sheryl, but he had never actually done it. Why? Well, it may have been because the bird only had one foot to shake with, and it was being used regularly for other things. Or it may have been for any number of other reasons, including the likely fact that Chester was just naturally deficient in brainpower. But whatever, he had never shaken hands.

So Travis, when he asked his goose to shake with the officer, didn't actually plan on it happening. He was just stalling for time, trying to think of something better to do, like instantly bailing out of the car.

You can imagine his surprise, then, when Chester suddenly hunkered down into his arms, flipped out his foot, and shook. Somehow that old Chestergoose always knew when the chips were down, and he rose in one way or another to the occasion. That day was no exception. Chester bobbed his head up and down a couple of times, hissed a little, and slowly raised his one black webbed foot toward the officer.

Well, that good man got a most unusual expression on his face, held it there for what seemed to be an eternity, blinked when Chester extended his foot even further, blinked again when the goose gave a soft honk, and actually grinned when Chester started clicking. And that was that. The officer was won.

With a roar of laughter that startled Travis much more than it did Chester, the man held out his hand, took hold of the webbed foot held in the air before him, and shook it. Then, still chuckling, he pulled his patrol car back onto the highway and he, Travis, and a goose called Chester were on their way.

For over an hour the officer asked Travis questions, wanting to know all about him, his parents, his brothers and sister, why he wasn't in school, and so on. But mostly the man was interested in the one-legged goose, and he listened intently as Travis told him about the bird and about his own commitment to teach him to fly.

When Travis had finished, the patrolman, whose name was George Pierpont, asked again the name of the doctor that the boy planned to visit. Then he got on his radio, and for the next fifteen minutes or so outlined Travis's story and his own desire to help, received approval to render assistance, and even made arrangements for Travis to meet the doctor.

Thus, early that afternoon a state highway patrolman, a small but determined boy, and a crippled goose paid a visit to one Dr. Steven Fielding, a specialist. That man, upon regaining his composure, listened attentively, made some notes, took some measurements, went over his schedule, wrote down directions to Travis's home, shook hands or whatever with Chester and Travis, winked at the patrolman, and promised Travis that he would see him within a week if he could, or within two weeks no matter what.

"Dr. Fielding?" Travis asked as they were rising to leave.

"Yes, son?"

"We need to talk about your pay. I . . ."

"Young man, we can discuss that later."

"But, sir . . ."

"No, Travis, I won't hear of it now. Let's see if I do any good. After that there will be plenty of time . . ."

At that point Officer Pierpont interrupted. "Excuse me, Doctor, but you ought to hear the boy out. He has a plan, and I think you'll like it. I know I would."

Dr. Fielding agreed, and so Travis reached into his pack and pulled out a picture which he had spent the previous month drawing.

"I know this ain't ... isn't money, but other than ten dollars in my savings account, it's all I've got. It's a pretty good picture of Chester, too. At least my mom says it is. Anyway, I'd sure like to trade it to you for your help. If it isn't enough, I ..."

Well, Dr. Fielding beamed, took the picture, told Travis it was more than enough, shook hands again all around, and saw the three to the door.

When Travis and Chester had gone out, Officer Pierpont turned back to the doctor and quietly spoke.

"Why are you doing this?" he asked.

For a long moment the doctor was silent, looking down at the drawing which he still held in his hand. "I suppose," he finally replied, looking up again, "it's the same reason that brings you here. Once in a while it's nice to be in the middle of something called love."

For a moment the two men looked at each other. Officer Pierpont then smiled and nodded, shook hands with the doctor once more, and walked out.

Later that evening, after having had a great afternoon with the boy and his goose, the patrolman pulled into the driveway of Travis's home, braked to a stop, and let the pair out of the car. Hank and Lois, who had been understandably worried, were horrified to see Travis brought home by a highway patrolman.

"Is everything all right?" Hank asked quickly, his voice filled with concern.

"Yes, sir," Officer Pierpont replied pleasantly as he watched Travis and Chester race across the yard. "Everything's just fine."

Then, climbing out of the car, he turned his gaze back to Hank and Lois. "Excuse me," he said quietly. "I'm Officer Pierpont, and I'm delighted to meet you folks. I've certainly heard a lot about you today."

"Today?" Hank questioned.

"Yes, sir. Travis and I have spent the day together. You're Hank, and of course you are Lois."

They all shook hands, and then the patrolman continued. "Before I go I'd like to suggest a couple of things to you. I know you have no idea where your boy has been today, but—"

"We did get a call from your office," Lois said, interrupting him. "We appreciated it, but to tell you the truth, I almost died when the girl told us she was with the highway patrol."

Officer Pierpont grinned. "I'll bet you did. We didn't mean to frighten you, but our calls occasionally do have that effect. Anyway, I'd suggest that you sit Travis down and teach him that hitchhiking is not only dangerous but is also illegal. I've told him that, but it helps if he knows that his parents understand it, too. That's the first thing.

"Secondly, I'd recommend that you not be too upset with the boy. Actually that was a pretty brave thing he did today. If I were you folks, I'd be proud of him. There's a lot of love in that little heart of his.

"Finally, I'd also appreciate it if you'd tell him, the next time he rides with me, to bring along a pet that's not quite so hard on my ears. I'll likely carry these dents for life."

Hank grinned. "If you think ears are bad," he chuckled, "you ought to have your nose tweaked a few times. There was once I thought I'd lost mine."

They all laughed quietly, and then the patrolman climbed into his car and backed out into the street. "Bye, Trav," he shouted as he pulled away. "Bye, Chester. I hope things work out for both of you."

A few moments later, when the excitement had subsided, curious children had been dispersed, and the chores were being attended to once again, Hank and Lois turned to their youngest son.

"Well?" Hank asked quietly.

"Well what?" Travis responded, grinning mischievously.

Hank and Lois looked at each other, and both were doing their best not to smile.

"For starters," Hank finally continued, "what does Officer Pierpont hope works?"

For an instant Travis hesitated. But then, grinning, he started up the stairs to change clothes. "Nothing, Dad," he replied as he ran. "Nothing. He was just being nice. Now, I'd better get to those chores, hadn't I?"

Travis turned the corner at the top of the stairs and was gone, and Hank and Lois were left alone, looking at each other and wondering.

"Do you ever have the feeling," Hank asked his wife, "that you really know nothing about your kids?"

"All the time," she replied quickly. "Almost every minute of my life."

"What do you suppose he did?"

Lois shook her head. "I don't have the faintest idea. Knowing his inclinations, though, I'm not at all sure I *want* to know."

Grinning, Hank put his arm around his wife. "I know what you mean. But remember, he inherited this from your genes, not mine, so you're the one who's really to blame."

"Wait a minute," Lois complained. "I'll have you know that—"

"Hey, I was just kidding," Hank said.

"Well, you'd better be. You're the creative genius around here, not me. I'm the practical one. Remember? His idea machine he got from you, strictly."

"All right, all right. But seriously, Lois, should I push this?"

"No ... I don't think so. Not after what the patrolman said. I have a feeling that we'll find out what he's done soon enough."

"Yes," Hank agreed. "I suspect you're right. Oh, well. Thank heaven he's all right."

"I'm going to," Lois stated sweetly as she reached for her husband's hand. "I'm going to get on my knees and do it right now. Would you care to join me?"

OCTOBER

Chapter 21
The Tractor

Hank was fond of teasing his boys by telling them that teenagers were just big loose nerve endings with super-activated embarrassment glands and low-level reasoning powers. The boys, of course, shrugged his comments off, but occasionally a situation arose where one or the other of them was forced to reconsider his father's words. Such a development occurred the day Jason finally asked Sheryl on a date.

Actually it wasn't much of a date, at least in terms of big expensive events. Jason planned on taking Sheryl to a movie, and prior to that, to Baskin-Robbins for ice cream. That was fine, and Sheryl seemed eager to go. The problem developed when he approached his father about taking the car. To Jason's frustration it was tied up, and the business car was not insured so that he could use it.

"Dad," he wailed, "I've got a date! I've already asked her. What am I going to do?"

Hank sat in the chair, his newspaper across his lap, gazing up at his eldest son. *How the boy has grown*, he thought. *Only a short time has passed since he was bouncing on my lap, and now he's dating and driving and working and the whole thing. In fact, sometimes he seems so consumed or preoccupied with things outside his family that I feel like adulthood has already claimed him. Oh, how fast life seems to speed by! If only I could have understood, when he and I were both younger . . .*

"Dad," Jason pressed, "how am I supposed to take Sheryl out without a car?"

"I don't know, Jase. I wish you had asked me a day or two earlier. Mom and I both have to use cars tonight, and I don't see any way out of it. Could you walk?"

Jason groaned. "Dad, you don't *walk* on a date! That's dumb!"

"Well, when I was a boy I walked! Lots of times I walked with your mother, and—"

"Yeah, and you also walked eighty miles to school through sixty feet of snow every day of the year."

About to lash out with anger, Hank looked quickly up at his son. But then he saw the slow grin spread across the boy's face, and slowly he relaxed.

"I guess you do hear that a lot, don't you?"

"Yeah," Jason responded. "It seems like it. I didn't mean to tease you, Dad, but I'm really worried about tonight. I honestly feel like I need a car, and I just don't know what to do."

"Take the tractor."

Both Hank and Jason spun around in surprise, for both had thought they were alone in the room.

"Travis," Hank called out, "where are you?"

"Here, trying to get warm on the heat vent behind your chair," the boy replied. Slowly then, he climbed to his feet and leaned on the back of his father's chair. "This is the warmest place in the house, and for a change I beat Steve to it. Jase, I think you ought to take the tractor."

"Oh, sure! Now that is far and away the dumbest . . ."

Hank raised his hand and put it on his oldest son's arm. "Wait a minute," he said thoughtfully. "That might be a good idea."

"Daaaad, no!" Jason anguished. "I couldn't ask Sheryl to do that! She . . . she'd freeze!"

"She'd like it, Jase," Travis said quickly. "She told me so."

"Oh, sure! When?"

"That day at the pond. She said she thought a date on the tractor would be fun."

"Well, Jase," Hank responded, "your problems seem to be solved. The tractor's free, and you have my permission to use it."

Well, Jason groaned like a stuck hog, but his options were before him and decision time had arrived. It was the tractor or walking, and wheels, no matter what their size or configuration, usually win out when it comes to a boy taking a girl on a date.

"All right," he finally mumbled. "I'll call Sheryl and tell her to dress warm. I sure hope she doesn't laugh at me, though."

"She won't," Travis said brightly. "I'm telling you, she told me she'd like it. I'll bet she really does."

Travis smiled widely at his older brother, Hank grinned and picked up the paper again, and Jason, after looking disgustedly at both of them, turned toward the kitchen and the telephone.

"Scrud," he murmured as he left, "my first date on a tractor. What a joke!"

As it turned out, Jason was right about one thing. It was cold! He was bundled up as tightly as he could get and he was still shaking worse than the old tractor. Sheryl, also bundled up in blankets as well as her coat, was seated on the wheel cover behind him, and he knew she was freezing, too. She had to be.

"Boy, this is embarrassing," he muttered to himself as he revved the old Ford up as high as it could go, desperately trying to hurry things along.

"What?" Sheryl shouted back at him. "I can't hear you!"

"I said, this is sure . . . Oh, never mind. Are you all right?"

Sheryl pulled her coat more tightly about her neck and did her best to stop shaking.

"Su-sure! Th-this is a riot."

Jason looked back to make sure he had heard right, responded with a weak grin to her smile and wink, and turned his gaze back to the road. Sheryl then leaned forward, put her hand on the boy's shoulder, and spoke into his ear.

"I'm glad you couldn't get your dad's car. This is really cool!"

"You mean cold?" Jason yelled.

"No," Sheryl laughed. "I mean a blast! You know, totally awesome."

Jason, very aware of the pressure of her hand on his shoulder, thrilled with the feeling of it, and, afraid to move lest she take it away, spoke rigidly.

"You . . . you sure? You really mean that?"

"Of course I do, silly. I'm going to write about th-this in my journal. My first date with J-Jason Tilby, on a tr-tractor. My grandchildren will love it!"

Well, Jason felt the red start creeping up his neck; he didn't know what to say, and so he stared at the road ahead and said nothing, hoping that Sheryl couldn't see his embarrassment. But she did, and he would have been even more embarrassed if he had seen what she did about it.

Over her smile of contentment she formed a kiss—a lingering kiss that her lips held and then repeated, a longing half-kiss that told the world how she felt about this boy who seemed to have become a part of her life.

The honk of a horn brought both of them back to reality, and seconds later, when Alec Suggins pulled alongside, slowed, and rolled down his window, they both wished they had gone elsewhere.

"Hey, Tilby," he shouted, while the boys in the car with him hooted and gestured, "I like your wheels! They're cool."

"Yeah," Jason responded, "they are at that."

"It must be the newest thing, plowing up a little turf with your date. But wait. You don't have a date. Not of your own. You have *mine*! And nobody plows turf with *my* girl!"

"Suggins," Jason shouted, "get lost! You're giving me a royal pain."

"I mean it, Tilby."

"So do I. Sheryl isn't your girl, and . . ."

Jason once again felt the pressure of Sheryl's hand on his shoulder, and then she, too, was yelling, telling Alec in no uncertain terms what she thought of him and of the people he surrounded himself with and of the way he conducted his life and of all the rotten things associated with it.

Alec, red with anger, slowed even more as he swung open his door. Jason also slowed down, and Sheryl suddenly realized that a fight was quickly shaping up.

"Alec?" she asked sweetly. "Do you know what I have with me under this blanket?"

The boy, still in his slowly moving car, looked blankly up at her.

"I have Travis's goose here," she continued. "As you may recall, he's a wild Canadian honker whose name is Chester, and you know how he feels about people who have the misfortune to be named Alec Suggins."

For a moment Alec stared, but then he decided to call the girl's bluff.

"You're lying," he snarled, "and I'm going to—"

"Get it," Sheryl finished for him. "One more step and I'm going to turn this bird loose on the whole bunch of you. Now, get lost before I do it!"

Well, you never saw anyone want so badly to do something and end up doing something else entirely. Alec knew Sheryl was bluffing, he really did. Thing was, his ear still seemed deformed from where the goose had nailed him months before, and he didn't want to feel that pain again.

Additionally, there was Jason Tilby, apparently ready and willing; and Alec had a great respect for his strength, so often exhibited on the playing field. No, maybe this wasn't the time . . .

Finally, humiliated once again before his friends, Alec snarled something about there being another day, and then he and his cronies were gone in a cloud of dust, leaving Jason and Sheryl sitting quietly on the tractor.

"What was that all about?" Jason finally asked. "How does he know about Chester?"

"They were introduced one day," Sheryl answered quickly, "and Alec never was very good at making friends."

"You don't have him in there, do you?"

"Chester?" Sheryl giggled. "Of course I do. I take him on dates with me all the time."

Jason smiled sheepishly. "You know," he said slowly, "that goose is really something. Even when he isn't here he's helping us."

"I know," Sheryl responded seriously. "And I'm just like Travis. I'm getting to the point where I really love that bird. Isn't it funny, though, how a goose can be so special and a human can be such a creep? Gosh but Alec's a lowlife."

"Yeah," Jason answered, finally grinning. "Maybe I shouldn't say this, but he reminds me of something my great-grandfather Hyrum used to say."

"What was that?"

"Well, according to what I've been told, he used to say that it's better to aim at the sun and miss than to aim at a pile of manure and hit it. Seems to me friend Alec's been aiming a mite low."

Sheryl giggled, Jason gently touched her hand for a moment, and then with a revving of the old Ford tractor's engine, they were off on their date again, both now ready to have the time of their lives.

Chapter 22
The New Foot

One week to the day from when Travis made his trip to the city, Dr. Steven Fielding drove into the Tilby driveway, climbed out of his car, and introduced himself to Hank and Lois. Then, while they watched in amazement, he walked to Chester's pen, lifted the strangely unprotesting bird out, shook the goose's foot in greeting, and then began fiddling with the other leg.

Finally satisfied, he placed Chester down, watched, picked the bird up and made a few more adjustments, and placed him on the ground again. Then he stepped back and grinned.

And there, to the amazement of both Hank and Lois, stood Chester, in all his fowled glory, on *two* good feet.

"Will it work?" Hank asked, still too surprised to ask anything else.

Dr. Fielding shrugged. "Who knows?" he answered slowly. "It just might. But even if it doesn't work for the goose, I have a feeling it'll work at least a little for your son."

"But how . . . how did you . . ." Lois began, her mind filled to overflowing with questions.

"Travis came to my office a week ago with Chester and a highway patrolman," the doctor answered. "I told him I thought I could help. I hope I have."

"But . . . but," Lois continued, "we can't pay you. I mean, I know those things are terribly expensive. How will we ever . . . ?"

"Mrs. Tilby," Dr. Fielding replied quickly. "You needn't worry about that. Travis has already paid me."

"He couldn't have," Hank stated. "He has no money but his savings, and I *know* that is still there."

"That's right," Lois agreed.

"I'd rather not explain further. Confidentiality between doctor and patient, you understand. But I will tell you that your son is a very talented artist. I hope you are encouraging him with that."

Lois, flustered, looked again at Chester, and for a long moment there was silence. Chester himself stood motionless, almost as if he was afraid to try his new prosthetic foot. At last, when the silence became uncomfortable, Hank spoke.

"Is that what kind of a doctor you are? I mean, one who does artificial limbs and so on?"

Dr. Fielding, grinning again, turned and walked to his car. Only after he had climbed inside, shut the door, and rolled down his window, however, did he answer. "Actually," he replied casually, "no, it isn't. I'm a gynecologist. But how do you explain that to a crippled goose and a boy filled with hope, especially when both have come so far?"

"But how on earth did he get *your* name?" Lois asked, feeling more confused than ever.

"I've no idea," the doctor replied seriously. "I only know how grateful I am that he did. That pair was like a breath of fresh air to me, and I'll be forever thankful that they came.

"Now I've got to get back. It's been a pleasure meeting both of you. Tell your son hello for me, and tell him also how much I hope Chester's leg works. God bless you both for raising such a son, and God bless him for . . . for believing in *me*."

And with that remark Dr. Fielding drove quickly away into the beauty of the morning, leaving Hank and Lois holding hands and watching him go, and feeling thankful, and wondering, really wondering.

Well, when school let out that day, things really started popping. Travis was ecstatic about the new artificial limb; and with Jason and Steve and Jenni encouraging and helping as best they could, and with Hank and Lois cheering from the sidelines, so to speak, Travis started putting Chester through flight training once again.

Only thing was, Chester could not get the hang of things. No matter how Travis pleaded and clicked and hissed and tried to communicate his thoughts to that big Canadian goose, nothing changed. Chester continued to hop on his one good foot, and he continued as well to think of the strapped-on limb as another confining rope, something to learn to escape from. Travis could find no way of telling the goose that he could use the prosthetic limb to walk and run on.

Day after day Travis arose early, worked with Chester, went to school, endured it, hurried home, and worked with Chester until long after dark. And, day after day, nothing changed except that it got nearer to Thanksgiving. The rope in the barn was forgotten entirely, Coach Gruninger's subtle harassment of Travis was ignored, Mrs. Sudsup's glowering stares whenever Chester was loose were not even noticed, good grades went out the window, and everyone in the Tilby family concentrated on getting Chester to fly.

Remember the old saying that a watched pot never boils? From what happened to Travis one would suspect there's some basis of truth to it. But whether or not that is so, it is true that quite often the things we want most to happen just don't. That's true no matter how much we want them, and even sometimes no matter how hard we pray. Chester's lack of flying ability was one of those inexorable issues, one of those relentless nonevents that defy all attempts to be altered. No matter what Travis or anyone else did or said, Chester simply could not run, could not get his large gray body into the air.

And then, to no one's surprise at all, Halloween arrived.

Chapter 23
The Pumpkin and His Lady

"Jason, you be careful!"

Patiently the boy turned back to his mother. "Mom, it's hard to be anything else on this dumb tractor."

"Well," Lois responded, "you be careful, anyway. A load of hay filled with kids isn't anything to fool around with."

"I won't, Mom. I promise."

Lois smiled and touched her son's hand. "I trust you, Jase. After all, everybody trusts the Great Pumpkin. Can I do less with you?"

Jason grinned and looked down at his bulging stomach, his costume for the Halloween dance. "It looks pretty awful, doesn't it?"

Lois nodded. "Is Sheryl's costume similar to yours?"

"Yeah, we planned them out, and she did them up on her sewing machine."

"Hey," Steve shouted from the wagon. "Let's go! I'm freezing!"

"Serves you right," Lois called back while Jason climbed stiffly onto the tractor. "You need a coat."

"Mom, have you ever seen a Thanksgiving goose in a coat?"

Lois smiled. "No, but the ones I've seen probably didn't wear long johns under their sparsely placed feathers, either. How're the Scarecrow and Mrs. King doing?"

"Mom," Travis groaned as he jumped to his feet. "He's not Mrs. King—he's Batman. Thing is, he doesn't like to wear his mask or anything else. He keeps picking at it and at his cape just like he picks at the rope and his new foot."

Lois smiled and encouraged her youngest son, and as she watched the tractor pull the wagon out of the yard she wondered again how it was that Travis and Chester could weave such a spell over her usual good sense. Actually she had agreed with both Jason and Steve; it *was* dumb to take a goose to a Halloween fair. But Travis had pleaded in his teasing yet pathetic sort of way, Chester had looked up at her with his soft black eyes, and she was won. Chester was on his way to the fair.

"Well," Hank said as Lois came back into the house, "that was four of a kind if I ever saw four of a kind."

"What do you mean?"

"Nuts. All of them. Three boys, one goose, and all four are nuts."

"Yes, but they're cute nuts, anyway. And Jenni's a fifth one: a fairy princess who must wait until

201

tonight to cast her spell. I hope we did the right thing, letting Travis take Chester."

"He'll be all right, Lois. Chester's eased up around people, and Travis doesn't have too much time left to be with his goose. I think it's a good idea, letting him build memories like this."

"I suppose it is, but I still worry."

"Of course you do. That's why you're such a good mother."

Lois looked up into her husband's face, snuggled into his arms, continued to worry, and fortunately had no idea at all about what was going to happen at the fair. Otherwise she'd have worried in earnest.

The school-sponsored Ellsworth Fair was held that year in the grove up at the Big Springs, and it was quite an event. It began with a hayride as three different wagons picked up youth and leaders, all dressed to the hilt in full costume for the occasion. Slowly the tractor-pulled wagons made their way up the steep and winding road to the Springs, while in the hay the kids sang and joked and jostled one another in halfhearted attempts to learn each other's identities.

Travis, of course, was easily identified because everyone had heard of Chester, and over and over he found himself and his goose the center of attention.

"Hey," someone shouted after the wagons were on their way, "it's Batman and Robin."

"No, it isn't," another giggled. "That thing's too big to be a robin. It's Batman and Strawman, the superheroes. I'd recognize them anywhere."

Everyone laughed, Travis grinned impishly, and

so it went, from one to another, all the costumes being joked about and admired.

Jason, bouncing along as the Great Pumpkin, was also known, as was Sheryl, who rode beside him on the wheel cover of the tractor. Other than that, however, few guessed each other's identities.

At the Springs, a PA system was blaring out square-dance music, and mounds of hamburgers, sacks of popcorn, and gallons of lemonade graced a long table near the large open tent, a treat for those who weren't exhilarated enough or filled by the music or by each other's company.

Chester, for instance, didn't like dancing much, and he was a lousy conversationalist. To Travis's dismay, however, he became an instant popcorn addict, creating quite a ruckus each time he hopped onto the popper. Of course it was funny at first, and lots of the kids offered him their food. But somehow the hoggish goose never got enough; and after a while kids and leaders started fighting him off.

For an hour or so Travis fought the bird himself, but finally the pint-sized scarecrow gave up and carried his hapless feathered companion back to the wagon.

"Boy," he growled as he plopped into the hay, "you are *really* a pain. I should have listened to Mother. Then I . . ."

And that was when Travis first noticed Alec Suggins and his two friends. They were not dancing, but were standing near the dunking pool, making fun of the little kids who were riding the two old donkeys.

"Hey, Chester," Travis muttered as he watched them, "what do you think's going on? I didn't see them on any of the wagons, and . . ."

Suddenly Alec Suggins pointed, and the larger of his two companions nodded. Quickly he left his buddies and made his way through the crowd, moving quickly toward some definite destination. For a moment, however, Travis lost sight of him, and so he turned his attention back to the others, but they were gone!

Searching back and forth across the crowd, Travis could see none of them. Slowly he climbed to his feet, hoping that the higher vantage point might help him to see better. He felt uneasy about those guys, though he had no idea why.

Reaching for Chester, Travis suddenly realized that the bird had slipped away. "Chester," he called. "Chester!"

Frantically Travis looked over the crowd, searching for his goose. But try as he would, he could not . . .

Suddenly, out of the corner of his eye, Travis saw a commotion. Spinning, he was horrified to see Alec and his buddies out in the field wrestling Chester into a large cardboard box.

"Jason!" Travis screamed as he leaped from the wagon and ran into the crowd of dancing teenagers.

"Jase, Steve, help!"

Jason and Steve stopped dancing and listened intently as Travis told of what he had seen. Instantly their partners were abandoned, and the three brothers turned and raced for the road. Suddenly they heard a car's engine turn over, and with a spinning of gravel and dirt, Alec Suggins's red convertible sped away into the trees.

"Jase," Travis screamed. "The tractor! Come on."

Seconds later, the three brothers clambered aboard the large red tractor, and soon they were chugging up the road with a yelling crowd right on their heels.

"Hang on, guys!" Jason yelled as he threw the tractor into gear. "We're going four-wheeling!" Even as he moved out, however, Jason was unsure. "We'll never catch them," he groaned. "On this stupid tractor there's just no way—"

"Hey," Steve cried out as he gripped one of the wheel covers to keep his balance, "don't give up so easily."

"Steve, have you seen how fast Alec's car goes? We couldn't catch him in a million years."

"Jase," Travis yelped as he did his best to hold on to the other wheel cover, "take a shortcut!"

"Yeah," Steve chimed in. "You don't have to follow no road. This is a tractor, remember?"

Well, Jason grinned, swung the wheel, a rusty barbed-wire fence quickly vanished beneath them, and they were headed downhill, the Great Pumpkin on his chugging steed, the feather-coated Steve beside him, and the straw-stuffed Travis on the other fender—together on this chase of chases. All in all it was a very interesting sight, as the fifty or so kids who were following on foot later testified.

The route they chose for their shortcut was rough and uncharted, but somehow through the trees they made their way forward.

Suddenly, above the other commotion, the three

205

boys heard another sound, a metallic grinding sound that they recognized.

"Jase," Travis shouted, "what's wrong?"

"The dumb thing's slipped out of gear, and I . . . I can't get it back in! We're in free-fall, I guess, and I—"

"Hit the brakes," Steve shrieked as he clung to the wheel covering. "Jase, hit the brakes and slow down!"

"I—I'm trying," Jason groaned as he pumped the pedals. "We must've busted a brake line or something. This thing's totally out of control!"

By then the tractor had picked up speed quite remarkably, the screaming crowd in the rear was dropping farther behind, and the rock-strewn hillside wasn't doing anything at all to make things smoother for the three heroes.

Travis and Steve were shouting pointless instructions, Jason was screaming at one or another of his brothers to get their fingers out of his eyes, and that crazy red tractor just kept rolling, faster and faster and faster. Frankly, between the tractor and its three screaming occupants, there was a whole lot of noise coming off that hill.

Jason, of course, never stopped doing his best to steer, but with his wide padded body bouncing around and thumping against him each time the tractor lurched over a rock, he didn't have much of a chance. Then, too, his brothers *were* grabbing him.

Just then the tractor slammed through an entire grove of scrub oak, and the straw-filled but pint-sized crusader was nearly torn from his precarious seat. Grabbing on to the wheel cover, he was just getting balanced again when Steve started hollering.

"Jase, Trav," he yelled almost incoherently, "we're gonna die! I don't wanna die! I'm too young . . ."

Jason and Travis both turned to try to soothe Steve, and at that instant the tractor bounced over a large rock and Travis was thrown off the wheel cover. With amazing slowness he sailed high into the air, drifted above Jason, and settled abruptly and really quite amazingly onto the hood of the tractor, driving the wind almost completely from his body.

Desperately he grabbed the metal and clung to it, breathing deeply, trying to catch his breath, knowing as he did so that the tractor was going faster than it ever had in all its born days and that Steve was right and they were all going to die and . . . and—

Squirming frantically, Travis wormed his way backward toward the steering wheel, knowing that it was pointless and that he was going to fall off and be crushed, but squirming anyway because he couldn't stop himself. But then Jason and Steve grabbed his legs and somehow he got around Jason and back onto the rear axle area near the wheel covers, where Steve deposited him none too gently in his old position.

"Thanks, Steve," he said as he looked up. "I . . ."

And then Travis saw, looming ahead, a stand of giant cottonwood trees with trunks that seemed to be about a hundred feet thick. For an instant that seemed forever, he was frozen with terror. He opened his mouth to scream and nothing came out. He moved his lips and tried again and still there was nothing. Finally, though, when only millimeters separated him and his brothers and the tractor from a low-lying limb that looked thirty feet thick, Travis found his voice.

"Look out!" he shrieked. "Hit the deck!"

And hit the deck (or axle) the three did. From that moment forward no one drove, and yet the tractor continued its desperate downhill plunge, anyway, seemingly controlled by a warped and twisted mind of its own.

For a second or two nothing happened, and then there was a terrific crash and tearing and ripping noise and the boys were being pummeled with branches and limbs; and then for an instant they were in the clear and the tractor was no longer bouncing but was moving smoothly and effortlessly, almost as if it were airborne.

And then there was another horrible crash and jolt, worse than all the others, and the tractor tentatively touched down (for it had indeed been doing a little flying), and finally it collided irrevocably with old Mother Earth, most likely never to leave it again.

That awful smashing wallop was followed by a bounce or two, another jolt, another crash, a horrid sound of groaning wounded metal crying out in pain; and suddenly the tractor and all about it were deathly still.

For a long moment there was total silence.

"Well," Steve groaned at last, "I guess I'm not dead."

"How do you know?" Jason gasped through clenched teeth.

" 'Cause I hear Travis breathing, and I know he's not going to heaven."

"What makes you think *you* are?" Travis responded painfully, and suddenly all three brothers began to laugh. It was a painful type of laugh, but it was a happy one because they were all more or less alive, and after an experience like they'd had, being alive was worth laughing about.

Gradually, as they groaned and moaned and giggled, the boys extricated themselves from the still upright and occasionally trembling tractor. All shook themselves, and each was amazed to discover that so far as he could tell he had no broken bones.

"Hey," Steve exclaimed as he stretched up to his full height for one final examination. "You know what? This is the road. We've gone and landed on the road! I wonder if . . ."

And then they all heard the roar of an approaching automobile engine, a roar that sounded suspiciously like the roar made by Alec's souped-up red convertible.

Well, poor Alec, for it surely was he. One can imagine his surprise when he roared around the corner with his buddies and his feathered kidnapped hostage, and found his path blocked by a beat-up old tractor, still quivering in the roadway. Hastily he slammed on his brakes and yanked his steering wheel to the side; and an instant later his cherry little car went over the embankment and slid to a stop on the very lip of a terrifying cliff.

When the dust finally settled, Alec and his friends had scrambled free and were standing on the road.

"Whew!" Alec declared. "I thought we were dead meat."

"One more foot," Tommy stated with a trembling voice. "That's all, man. One more foot and we would have been."

"Hey!" Travis suddenly yelled. "Where's Chester?"

Before anyone could stop him, Travis leaped the embankment and slid toward the teetering car. "Chester," he cried as he scrambled downward. "Hang on! I'll get you out of there!"

With rocks and dirt and other debris sliding after him, Travis skidded to a stop against the dusty side of the convertible. The deep gorge yawned before him, and Travis, his heart in his throat, hesitated. But then from within the car, he heard a soft clicking, and he hesitated no longer.

"Chester," he called as he carefully opened the door. "Chester! I . . ."

"Hey!" Alec yelled from up above. "You be careful with my car, you little creep."

"Don't yell at my little brother," Steve snarled.

"You'd yell, too, if your car was on the edge of a cliff like that. My old man is going to kill me when he finds out what has happened."

"Hey," Tommy exclaimed, "how 'bout Delaney's winch? We could haul it back up with the winch."

"Yeah," Alec said, "we could if . . ."

Travis, meanwhile, had finally taken hold of the box. When he pulled at it, the car suddenly groaned and teetered forward. With a gasp of fear,

Travis froze. Loose rocks ground their way from under the car and rattled into the gaping canyon below.

"Come on, Chester!" Travis whispered, trying to calm himself as much as his goose. "It's now or never. Let's do it!"

With a mighty yank, Chester's cardboard prison was pulled free from the back seat of the car.

Desperately Travis lunged uphill with the box and Chester securely in his arms.

Suddenly, with a grinding creak, the car teetered forward and hung for a moment as though ready to fall. Strangely, however, it stopped again, and there was no sound on the hill.

"You little jerk!" Alec screamed from above. "Get away from my car!"

"Travis," Jason called, "are you all right?"

"Yeah," Travis gasped. "I'm okay . . . I'm coming up."

"Tell him to be careful around my car," Alec shouted fearfully.

Travis, starting upward with Chester in his arms, suddenly slipped and slid back down toward the car.

"Trav, be careful!" Steve yelled down.

"I am," Travis grunted. "I slipped on this stupid hubcap."

Disgusted, Travis lifted the hubcap and threw it down the hill behind him. Then he watched as the hubcap bounced and then slammed into the open door of the car.

Resuming his climb, Travis was not even watching when the car, impelled by the slight impact of the hubcap, teetered off balance, lurched, gained momentum, and suddenly disappeared over the gaping edge of the cliff.

All in all, it seemed a very just way to end a Halloween fair.

Chapter 24
Everybody Learns

In spite of everything that all of the Tilbys had done to make amends for Chester having eaten Mrs. Sudsup's prize flowers, that woman was not about to forgive. Nor would she forget the humiliation she had suffered at church because of her feathered enemy, nor at the Tilby home because of Travis. As far as she was concerned, Chester was evil incarnate; Travis and by association all of the Tilbys were evil, too, and nothing would change her mind.

When Hank and Lois finally realized how deeply her feelings went, they poured on the love, so to speak, by being as kind to her as they could. Then they encouraged Travis to avoid going near her property, especially if he had Chester with him.

Travis and all of the Tilby kids were usually obedient, for they had learned by experience how painful it was to be otherwise. Occasionally, however, something happened, and one or another of them forgot or simply made a poor decision, leaving broken rules scattered all over the place. That night, after they were finally home from the Halloween dance, Travis made such a choice. He dragged Chester's pen across the October-dead orchard so that the goose could be on clean ground.

There was an apple tree there that he wanted Chester to clean up beneath, which was good. Those particular apples, though, were supposed to be for the pigs; Travis knew it, and in that decision he was being downright disobedient. To be fair, however, he really did forget how close the apple tree was to Mrs. Sudsup's property and house; and that part of his disobedience was purely a forgetful mistake. But whichever, the results were the same. The Tilby family went to bed unawares; and Chester, the mortal enemy of Mrs. Sudsup, was left within just a few feet of the Sudsup fence and master bedroom.

Nobody ever found out how the fire started, and it probably didn't matter. What mattered was that it did some pretty interesting things before it was put out. One of those things had to do with Chester.

The first Travis knew of the fire, though he didn't know it was fire at the time, was when he became aware that Chester was making a terrible racket outside in his pen.

Travis staggered from his bed, saw that it was almost five-thirty in the morning, and then once more realized that the terrible noise he was hearing was coming from outside, and in fact was coming directly from his pet.

Hurriedly pulling on his boots and coat, the boy leaped down the stairs and sprinted across the kitchen, totally unaware that his brothers and parents had also awakened. With his heart in his throat he threw open the door, raced across the frozen ground, circled the house, and headed for Chester's pen.

Chester was literally acting like he had gone crazy; and Travis, even after he arrived at the pen, could not understand why. First Chester hopped in one direction, flapping his giant wings and honking uncontrollably. After he had slammed into the side of the pen, he changed directions and did the same thing over again somewhere else.

Quickly Travis opened the door to the pen and lifted his bird out. Then, with gentle clickings and hissings, he did his best to calm the goose's ruffled feathers. Only, Chester didn't want to calm down, not for sour apples he didn't. Over and over he lunged to get away from the boy, and so finally, reluctantly, Travis complied with the bird's obvious wishes.

Bending down, he set the goose upon the ground, and he was just starting to try to gentle him again when the large fowl, thoroughly upset, squirmed free of the boy's hand and noisily departed.

The early morning sky was gray with dawn. As he stared in open-mouthed amazement, Chester spread his wings and fled straight away, hopping from his real foot to the prosthetic one and back again, gaining momentum—actually *running!*

"*Chester!*" Travis shrieked, his voice filled with shock and wonder. "Dad! Mom! Hey, everybody!

Anybody! Look at Chester! He's running! He *really* is!''

And then Hank and Lois were beside their son, ignoring him, staring at the burning flames that were entirely filling one room of the Sudsup house.

As Travis watched, horrified, Chester slammed into the fence that separated the properties, honking and making the most terrible racket the boy had ever heard. Back and forth Chester ran, his feathers puffed out and his great wings flapping, away from the house and back toward it, almost as if he were fighting the fire itself, almost as if he were considering running into it. *But he can't*, Travis thought.

"Chester!" he screamed. "No! Get away . . ."

A window suddenly broke on the downstairs level of Mrs. Sudsup's home; and as fire immediately began licking up the outside wall, Travis became aware of two things at once.

The first was that his father and brothers were already dragging out the hose from the garage and hooking it up so that they could fight the fire. The second was that there was a figure in the upstairs window, a figure waving frantically for help.

Travis, as he turned to run for the garage and the ladder that was there, saw Chester once more as the big bird slammed again into the fence below Mrs. Sudsup's window. For an instant he was grateful that the bird couldn't fly, and that was the last he even thought of his pet. He was, quite frankly, too busy to think much about geese as he hauled out the ladder and steadied it for his father to rescue Mrs. Sudsup.

Well, the next hour was pretty frantic, and a whole lot of things happened that don't need to be described here. However, the fire *was* contained and put out by Mrs. Sudsup, the Tilbys, and, finally, the volunteer fire department; and surprisingly it damaged only the kitchen and living room on the downstairs level of her home, plus a little of the outside wall.

Sunrise found them all, the Tilbys and Mrs. Sudsup and the police and the man who was captain of the fire department, in the Tilby kitchen. There they were getting dry and warm from icy sprayed water and holding an informal inquest into the cause of the fire.

As was mentioned earlier, that cause was never discovered; but what was discovered, or at least pointed out (and this by a contrite Mrs. Sudsup herself), was that Chester's noise, made most likely because he so feared or hated fire, was the one single factor that had awakened her and saved her life.

Well, you never saw anybody do so much apologizing as she did, and you never saw anybody enjoy an apology so much as Travis enjoyed hers. Altogether it was pretty wonderful, for Mrs. Sudsup was suddenly the Tilbys' neighbor again, Travis and the rest of them were once more good people, and Chester could actually run. And frankly it seemed like a pretty good way to start the first day of November.

NOVEMBER

Chapter 25
The Goose Gets Stubborn

Isn't it funny how, when everything looks like it's going to work out like we want it to, it doesn't? No one really understands why that's so—unless it's a part of Murphy's law or something—but still it seems to be true, and a lot of us suffer because of it.

Travis experienced that old law firsthand the day after the fire, November first, when he tried to get Chester to run again. He put the bird on the ground, encouraged him patiently, and finally even yelled with frustration, but it did no good. Chester simply would not use his new leg.

The goofy bird wouldn't even use it when everyone in the family started chasing him, yelling and kicking at him and doing all they could to drive him away. Chester seemed to think they had invented a new game, and he joined in with vigor, honking and chasing the Tilbys as much as they were chasing him, hopping along on his one foot just like always.

It's likely that if someone had been watching, they would have thought it looked funny, but it was anything but that, at least to Travis and his family. Thanksgiving was only a little more than three weeks away, and Chester had to get into the air and leave for good if he was going to live. So all joined in, doing what they could, and hoping and praying that Chester would go.

They threw the big bird into the air again, over and over; and Chester simply came back down. Steve ran with him, holding the goose out in front, fighting off flapping wings and goose down in his eyes and mouth and running until he had made a literal trail through the pasture. But even that didn't help. Travis climbed the barn again, with a honking goose under his arm; and standing on the ridge he threw the bird out into space. For a moment that finally seemed to work, for Chester lifted his wings, flapped them sort of, and soared with ungainly progress across the yard. When he landed, however, there was an ungainly flapping, a great stumbling on a foot and an artificial limb, and a final confusing collision between bird and ground. Chester maybe had run once, but he'd certainly never mastered the art of flying or landing.

Days passed, then a week, then two, and still nothing changed. No matter what they did or did not do, Chester would not fly. Travis lost sleep and wouldn't eat; Hank and Lois worried and prayed constantly about him and about his pet; the other family members schemed and planned and worked; and *still* nothing changed.

"Mom," Travis asked the Friday afternoon before Thanksgiving, "what's the matter with him? He won't even try!"

Lois, putting away the dishes Travis had just dried, looked down at her small son. Reaching out, she pulled him to her and held him close while her heart ached with sorrow for him.

"I know," she finally answered. "There are probably lots of reasons why he won't, but probably the main one is that he loves you."

"But, Mom, if he loves me, he'll go. I don't want him to stay around here and die!"

Lois smiled. "I know that, Trav, and you know it. But Chester's only a goose. How can he know he's going to die if he stays? All he knows is that you're you and that you've always done the best things for him. He loves you because he knows you care. I don't blame him, either. I wouldn't want to leave a wonderful person like you."

"Aw, come on, Mom. Be serious!"

Lois hugged her son again. "I am serious, Trav, but still, I think I know how you feel."

For a moment there was silence, and then suddenly Travis swung free.

"I know," he exclaimed. "I'll take him out and turn him loose in the field. Mr. Larson will think he flew away, and then if he finds his way back here, well, what can a kid say?"

"Trav," his mother asked quietly, "what's 'a blinken'?"

"Mom," the boy pleaded, "that's not being dishonest. I wouldn't lie. I just wouldn't tell everything."

"Would Abe Lincoln do that?"

"Aw, how do I know what he'd do? He probably never faced anything like this, anyway."

Lois turned, picked up another dish, and reached to put it away. "No," she said quietly, "he probably never did. When he was President, though, he watched hundreds of thousands of Americans die because of a decision he'd made, a decision he'd made because his conscience told him it was right. I imagine that was pretty hard, don't you?"

Travis slowly nodded, his eyes downcast. "Well," he replied gloomily, "maybe he did. But anyway, I'm not Abe Lincoln!"

"No, you aren't, but you *are* Travis Tilby, and that makes you one of the finest people I've ever had the honor of knowing. Now, come on. Stop feeling sorry for yourself, or for Chester, and start exercising your faith. God expects that of you. And frankly, young man, I expect nothing less from you myself."

Well, Travis grinned weakly, stood up, and walked to the door. "Mom," he said as he opened it to go out, "would it be wrong if I took Chester to the field tomorrow, anyway, just to see if he'll fly when he gets there?"

Lois, smiling widely, threw the dish towel at her son. "Get out of here," she said, laughing. "You've got until next Tuesday. Until then, anything goes, including, I hope, Chester."

Chapter 26
Off the Cliff

It was Monday, the week of Thanksgiving, school was out for the day, and Jason and Sheryl were standing and watching while Steve once again ran with the goose. Travis and Jenni were seated on a nearby log, totally caught up in wanting Chester to fly.

"Why is Steve running with him?" Sheryl suddenly asked, turning to look up at Jason. "How will that help?"

"We're not sure," the boy answered resignedly. "But to fly Chester's got to have speed, and he won't run and pick up any himself. Trav has done everything possible and then some, and Chester *still* won't use his new leg. They hope that by running, they'll give Chester some speed and he'll get the hang of moving fast through the air."

Sheryl turned again to watch the speeding boy, and Jason looked down at her. A random breeze suddenly picked up a wisp of her hair and tossed it across her face; and Jason, seeing it, thought again of how pretty she was. It was amazing, he thought, that she actually liked him. Of course he liked her, too, an awful lot, but still she made him nervous. That was because she was so . . . so . . . well, just neat was the word he guessed he wanted.

Again the wind moved her hair, and he longed to reach out and brush it back. Only he didn't, and he knew he wouldn't—ever. That would take more nerve than three of him might have. Of course he'd held her hand a couple of times, but contrary to what he'd said teasingly to his parents, he'd never done anything more. He'd thought of kissing her, thought of it maybe a million times, in fact. Only he hadn't, and . . . well, doggonnit, if he only had more nerve . . .

"I feel bad," Sheryl suddenly said. "Trav was counting on me to help with Chester, and I haven't been around a lot, especially lately. I should have come to help him more often."

"Yeah," Jason responded, "that would have been great."

Sheryl turned and looked up at him, her eyes large and soft, and Jason suddenly realized there was more than one interpretation to what he had said.

"I . . . I mean," he stammered, his face growing more red by the second, "that I . . . ah . . . I mean Travis could have really used your . . . I mean . . . it would have been great for Travis, uh . . . and I like you to be around, too, and . . . er, ah . . ."

Sheryl, doing her best not to giggle, turned

quickly away. "Has Chester ever used it?" she asked, interrupting Jason's stammerings. "His artificial leg, I mean."

"Yeah." Jason breathed with relief, grateful that Sheryl had not noticed his discomfiture. "Once. He used it the morning Mrs. Sudsup's house caught on fire. He *hates* fire, and when he saw her house burning, he kind of went crazy. He was running all over the yard. I only saw him once, but—"

"Jason," Sheryl interrupted, "maybe it was the fire that made him run."

"Yeah," the boy responded absently, "maybe it was."

"You're not listening to me, Jason. If fire made him run three weeks ago, wouldn't it do the same thing now?"

Jason looked down at Sheryl in surprise. "I don't know," he replied slowly. "It might. Yeah, it just might!

"Hey, Trav! Come here! Quick! Sheryl had an idea that sounds pretty good. In fact, it sounds great."

And that was how the Tilby kids, with the aid of Sheryl's impeccable logic, found out how to make Chester run. And he did, too, like crazy. Travis built a fire on a bare spot down at the bottom of the pasture; and when Chester saw it, the poor bird went berserk. Immediately his feathers puffed out, his wings spread, his head lowered and darted forward, his wild honking began, and suddenly the goose was moving.

Like an avenging angel he charged the fire, running, actually using both legs in his haste to get at it. Travis stared in disbelief as the goose ran, and then with a frantic squeal the boy took off, trying to head Chester off before the crazy goose raced into the flames.

"Chester!" he screamed. "No! Don't go . . ."

And with a last-minute lunge he reached the goose and pushed him aside. Chester, though, was not to be thwarted that easily. With a furious honking and clicking he raced around Travis and ran once again at the fire. Travis lunged again and missed, and Chester would probably have burned his feathers pretty badly had not Steve, at the last possible second, thrown a cross-body block on the goofy bird.

Jason, just arriving, grabbed the struggling fowl, and together the brothers carried him off and out of sight of the fire.

"My gosh," Travis gasped as he sat down with the bird in his lap, "can you believe what fire does to him? Why do you suppose that's so?"

Steve shrugged his ignorance, but Jason had a theory. "Remember how he attacked that rattler, Trav?"

The boy nodded, and Jason went on.

"Maybe it's instinct. Maybe it's like Mr. Larson said, that he lost his leg in a fire. I don't know for sure, but that could be it. Anyway, I'll bet Chester thinks fire is an enemy he can attack just like he did that snake."

Travis nodded his head. "Maybe so. It's sure weird, though. I thought animals were supposed to be afraid of fires."

"They usually are," Steve suddenly said. "But I really don't think it matters."

"What do you mean?"

"Look, you goofballs, Chester *ran*! The fire, for whatever reason, made him do it. Both times. Who cares if he's supposed to? Now all we have to do is get him to run faster, beat his wings a little harder, and presto, he'll fly."

"Do you really think so?" Travis asked hopefully.

"Sure he will," Jenni said quickly. "Tomorrow's the last day, so it's got to work, just like in my storybooks."

Well, the boys groaned, Sheryl smiled tenderly and hugged the little girl, and Jenni reached up and held Sheryl's hand.

"You're pretty when you smile," the little girl said quietly. "I think I love you just like Jason. Are you going to marry him?"

Sheryl blushed crimson, Jason started squirming again, Travis found something on one of Chester's feathers to study, and Steve coughed and stared up at the sky. Altogether it was a pretty embarrassing moment for everyone there—everyone, that is, but Jenni.

"Uh . . . well, let's try it again," Jason suddenly said, hoping by that to escape the mortifying situation his little sister had so innocently created. "Steve's fastest, so let him run alongside Chester toward the fire. That way he can steer him away from it."

"All right," Steve replied easily. "I'll try that. But how're you going to get him to flap his wings?"

"I'll show him how," Jenni replied quickly. "I'll

go down by the fire and show him how while he's running toward me."

There was silence as each of them mentally laughed at Jenni's plan. Finally, though, Jason spoke. "The trouble with an idea like that," he said, grinning, "is that nobody seems to have a better one. Okay, Jen. You and Sheryl go down by the fire; I'll stand somewhere along the route; Trav, you let him go; and Steve, you run like crazy. Come on. Let's do it!"

They did, and Chester ran again. In fact, he ran like a goose gone mad. The trouble was that he paid no attention to Jenni's frantic waving. He was concentrating on that fire, and flying was the last thing in his fowled-up mind.

Finally, exhausted from several attempts that had about wiped him out, not to mention what they had done to Chester, Steve dropped to the ground.

"Scrud," he groaned, "this is never going to work. Sheryl, come on. Let's hear another one of your great ideas."

"Steve," Jason warned, "you'd better be—"

"Hey," Sheryl quickly interrupted, "it's okay. He didn't mean anything bad. He's just discouraged, exactly like the rest of us."

Steve looked at her gratefully, and Sheryl quickly smiled at him. Then, with almost no pause, she went on.

"I've been thinking, though," she observed, "that Chester does everything but get into the air."

"We know that," Travis said quietly. "It's been

the same way since July, or whenever it was when he got big enough to fly."

"No, it hasn't, Travis," Sheryl argued. "Not exactly. He's only been running on his own, really running, since today. But anyway, have you thought about throwing him off something high?"

"Yeah," Jason responded quietly. "We've tried that. We threw him off the barn a dozen times. Nothing happens except that the fall about kills the dumb thing."

"Jase," Jenni complained, "quit calling him that. Gooses aren't dumb."

"I'm sorry, Jen. It's just hard to imagine why it's so difficult to teach a *bird* how to *fly*. I'll bet we've spent a thousand hours on Chester, and it's just like pounding sand down a —"

"Jase," Travis suddenly shouted, "that's it!"

"What's it?" the older boy asked, surprised.

"Sand! The Sand Cliffs, up the canyon!"

Well, everyone looked at each other, and there is no doubt that all of them thought poor Travis had finally lost a screw and fallen off the shelf. From the way he was acting he'd come loose from the wall, for sure, and there was no doubt about it at all.

"Little brother," Steve finally said, "you're making very little sense."

"I am, too," the boy avowed. "Just listen to me. Let's take Chester up on top of the Sand Cliffs, start a fire on the edge, and run him off."

"But, Trav," Jenni wailed, "that's a long way down. Chester'll get hurt and maybe even die."

"I know that, Jen. But he'll die anyway, tomorrow. I think Chester'd want to try it, especially if he knew what his future was going to be otherwise. Don't you?"

Jenni, her head down, nodded. And so in less time than it takes to tell about it, the plan was relayed to Hank and Lois. Permission was given for Jason to take the car, and within minutes all were ready to start.

Jenni, much to her dismay, was ordered to stay at home, but Travis consoled the little girl by telling her that he'd say good-bye to Chester for all of them once the goose was in the air. Wiping her tears away, she agreed, hugged Chester, and then stood in the road watching as the car sped away. Travis thought of her all the way out of town, and he felt bad about leaving her behind. So did the others, for at one time or another all mentioned it; and Travis was impressed that the older boys were starting to show their love for their little sister.

Soon, however, all else was forgotten as the three brothers, Sheryl, and an unusually quiet Chester sped up across the divide toward Salt Creek Canyon and the strangely shaped sand formation known locally as the Petticoat Cliffs.

It was almost sundown when Jason pulled the car to a stop on the bumpy road at the bottom. Slowly then, they all climbed out of the car and stared up at the towering ramparts.

"Gosh," Travis stated solemnly, "I didn't know they were that high."

"I did," Jason commented. "I've climbed them. Well, how do you want to do this? We've got to hurry or it'll be dark."

Travis leaned over and lifted Chester in his arms. "Is there an easy way up?" he asked.

"Yeah," Jason responded. "Around the side. It's longer, but it's a whole lot safer. That's the way I think we should go."

"Okay, lead the way, and let's do it."

"Uh . . . Jason," Sheryl said slowly, "I don't think I should go up there."

"Why?"

"I don't think my folks would like it if they found out."

"All right, but I don't feel good about leaving you here alone, either."

"I'll be okay."

"I'm sure you will, but I still don't like the idea. I think I'd better stay here, too. Steve, what do you think? Can you and Trav find the way up?"

Steve looked up at the cliffs. "Sure," he replied. "That way I can run with Chester."

"No," Travis answered quickly. "I want to do it. I can't do it as fast as you, but maybe Chester won't need to go that fast. Maybe he just needs to get out in the air."

"Okay," Steve agreed, "he's your bird. But let's hurry. Like Jase said, it's going to be dark pretty soon."

For the next little while the two boys made their way up the steep but climbable hill behind the cliffs. They took turns carrying Chester, who made little fuss, and they finally got to the top just as the sun reached the horizon. They located a place that was flat, and Steve set about building a fire. Travis, meanwhile, moved Chester to the other side of a small hill, where he waved down at Jason and Sheryl, who were standing far below.

After that one short look, however, Travis quickly moved back from the edge of the cliff. It was a long way down, an awfully long way, and just standing there looking and waving made him dizzy. How could he ever force Chester off the edge? he wondered. What if the goose couldn't fly? What if he were killed in the fall? Travis couldn't bear the thought of that happening. Oh, the whole thing was crazy! Why had he thought of this? Why had he ever agreed to raise the dumb goose in the first place? Nobody needed twenty dollars that badly.

"Chester," he whispered, burying his nose in the goose's breast, "I'm sorry to do this to you. Maybe I shouldn't. Maybe I should just climb back down . . ."

"Trav," Steve called. "The fire's about ready. Hurry!"

Travis hurriedly dropped his head and closed his eyes. "Dear God," he whispered, "please don't let my goose die. Please? Just make a miracle and help him to fly. He's got good wings, and he's real strong, so it won't even need to be a very big miracle. I ain't, I mean, I haven't asked for much, ever, and if you do this, I promise I'll be real good for . . . for all the rest of my life! Amen."

Opening his eyes and drying them on his sleeve, Travis took a deep breath and hugged his goose even more tightly. "Chester," he whispered again, trying as he did so to blink back the tears that were already filling his eyes. "I . . . I guess this is good-bye. Thanks for being my fr-friend. You're great, and I mean it! And remember, no matter what happens out there, I l-love you! Now, come on! Get out there and *fly*!"

The goose took a nip at the boy's ears, and then, before he had time to think further, Travis ran over the hill and showed Chester the fire.

Chapter 27
Different Views

After his brothers had gone, Jason did his best to make Sheryl comfortable while they waited. They sat on opposite fenders of the old car; and when they weren't talking, they listened to the sighing of the cold wind through the junipers, the only other sound on the mountain. It was a lonely spot where they waited, lonely but lovely, and Jason was glad that his brothers had not minded that he wanted to stay with Sheryl.

Getting Chester to fly was important, but so was Sheryl; and somehow, no matter how much time he spent with her, it never seemed to be enough. That was why Jason was thankful that he had this new chance to be alone with her. And to him, now, that seemed just as important.

Cautiously he looked over at her, once again studying her features. She was leaning back on her stiffened arms, gazing up at the cliffs; and the sun, dropping now below the heavy cloud layer, was splashing its golden light across her face. Her long hair was dancing in the wind, and Jason thought surely she was the most beautiful creature in the whole world.

"Do you think he'll fly?" the girl asked suddenly.

Jason, feeling guilty for staring at her, looked up at the cliff above them. "I don't know," he replied honestly. "I really want him to, but I sure don't know if he will."

"I think he will," Sheryl said, turning toward him and smiling. "I really do."

"Why?"

"Because everyone's done so much praying about it."

"How do you know that?"

"Jenni told me. And since then I've been praying about it, too. God has answered my prayers lots of times, and I hope he does now. Besides," she added, smiling, "how could anybody, especially God, turn down someone as cute as Jenni?"

Jason looked at the girl with new appreciation, wondering how she managed to discuss such private things without any show of anxiety or embarrassment. She was really something. What bothered him, though, was why she liked him, or maybe not that so much as how it had happened. One day she had been Alec's girl, and the next day she had been his, or at least sort of. And he couldn't figure out how that had worked. He'd done nothing, nor had anyone else that he knew of.

"Uh . . . Sheryl, can I ask you something?"

Quickly the girl looked over at him, her face

236

serious. "Sure," she replied. "I hope I can answer it."

"Yeah. Me, too. I was just wondering what . . . uh . . . how come . . . uh, oh, shoot, how come you aren't Alec's girl anymore?"

"Was I ever?"

"Well, yeah, or at least I guess so. Everybody said you were."

"Including Alec?"

"Yeah, sure. He talked about you all the time. He was always bragging about how you and he . . . uh . . . about the two of you."

"Did you believe him?"

"Not much. Alec likes to brag. He always has. Except for the part about your being his girl, I just figured that's what he was doing."

"And you really thought I was his girl?"

"Well, sure. You were always with him, and . . ." Sheryl turned her face away, pulled her coat collar more tightly around her neck, and looked back up at the cliff. "I guess," she said slowly, "that anybody would have thought that. It certainly must have looked that way."

"Well, weren't you?"

"Jason," she said, looking again at him, "have you ever been trapped, where you got into something almost by accident and you couldn't get out?"

Jason grinned. "Yeah, whenever I tell a lie. Then I have to tell another one to cover up the first one, and another and another; and that's like a trap. Before long I've told so many I get confused and get tripped up. I guess I just don't have a good enough memory to be a good liar."

Sheryl giggled delightedly. "That's exactly what I mean. And I know what you're saying, too. I can't lie, either. But, Jason, that's what happened with me and Alec. I got trapped. He gave me a ride home from school one day; and I thought I was pretty neat, riding home with a boy in a car. All my friends were jealous, and I was really proud. He gave me a ride the next day, too, and the next, and before long I didn't know how to tell him no. Sometimes I really wanted to go somewhere with my friends, but I couldn't even do that anymore. I mean, I probably could have, but I didn't know how, or maybe I didn't dare, or something. Anyway, I was trapped."

"So how did you get out of it?" Jason asked quietly. "Why did you even want to? Alec's rich, he's a jock, he has a classy car, he—"

"Jason," Sheryl said softly as she reached across the car hood to take his hand, "Alec is the opposite of you in all the important ways, and that's why I didn't want to be with him any longer. He's mean and he's selfish, and I don't think people ought to be that way. You aren't."

Embarrassed, Jason dropped his gaze. "So . . . uh . . . how did you get out of it, being his girl, I mean?"

"You don't know?" Sheryl asked, surprised. "Didn't Travis tell you?"

"Tell me what?"

"About that day down at Les Simms's pond?"

"Was *that* the day?"

Sheryl nodded silently.

"Uh . . . he tried," Jason explained, "but this

238

person you think is so kind and unselfish wouldn't listen to him. I called him a liar when he told me he'd walked home with you, and he wouldn't tell me anything else, not that I blame him. I don't even know what happened that day."

Sheryl smiled and squeezed his hand. "See," she said, "you're honest, too, even when it hurts. That's another thing I like."

Jason, now more embarrassed than ever, stared up at the cliff while Sheryl talked about the day at the pond. "And it was when Chester got ahold of Alec's ear," she said finally, "that I decided it was all over between us."

"Chester got Alec's ear?" Jason asked, grinning widely.

Sheryl giggled. "Uh-huh. And it was the funniest sight you ever saw! Alec couldn't get away, and he was yelling and carrying on like a little kid. Chester took care of him like nobody has for years."

"Boy, I believe it! That dang bird got my finger once, and I thought I was going to lose it."

"You shouldn't have been mean to him. He only bites people who have been mean to him."

"Or mean to Travis," Jason added ruefully.

"Yes, that's true. I really believe Chester and Travis love each other. And when I saw how they protected each other, then I *knew* I had to get to know them!"

"So you really weren't interested in . . . in me?"

Quickly Sheryl looked over at Jason. "Silly," she answered seriously. "Certainly I was interested in you. Lots of girls are. But you're so stuck up that—"

"I am not! I'm just . . . well, doggonnit, I'm bashful!"

"You?" the girl responded teasingly. "Come on."

Jason was now starting to turn red. He could feel it; and no matter what he did, he didn't know how to stop it. All he could hope for was that Sheryl couldn't see it.

"It's true," he finally declared, wishing that she'd stop watching him and smiling.

"Well," she asserted, grinning, "it's hard to tell the difference, except that you *do* look good in red."

Now Jason really started to blush, and he was wishing with all his heart that he had climbed the cliff and left Steve behind to look after Sheryl.

"And so," Sheryl concluded softly, doing her best to ease the boy's obvious discomfort, "when I realized how sweet Travis and Chester were, I decided that you would probably be the same way. My parents tell me that good qualities like that run in families. They were right, and incidentally, so was I. But I *really* didn't think you liked me. Of course Travis told me otherwise, but—"

"He *what*?"

"Trav told me that you liked me."

"What else did he say? About me, I mean."

"Oh," Sheryl answered, smiling mischievously, "lots and lots of things."

"Like what?"

"Golly, Jason," the girl responded teasingly, "I could *never* tell you. I'd be too embarrassed."

"Well, that little bounder," Jason growled. "When he gets back down here, I'll . . ."

"You do, don't you?"

"Huh?"

"Like me?"

"Uh . . . yeah," Jason replied, suddenly waxing bold. "I like you lots! Do you like me?"

"Well, of course I do, silly. I already said that. I like anybody who's related to Travis and Chester."

"Trav and Chester?" Jason asked, confused. "But I thought—"

"Jase," Sheryl cried as she jumped down from the car. "Look! There's Trav up there, and Steve, too. See? He's waving!"

Eagerly she began waving; and Jason, jumping off the car himself, waved as well. Then, in silence, they watched as Steve quickly put together a small fire on the edge of the cliff.

By the time it was burning brightly they were standing in cold shadow, though the sun still gilded the sandy cliffs above. Sheryl, wrapping her arms about herself, shivered in the November chill; and Jason longed with all his heart for the courage to put his arm around her and help her to keep warm.

"Look," she whispered, "Steve is going behind those trees."

"Yeah," Jason responded, "he's hiding so he won't distract Chester. That means they're ready. Gosh, I hope this works."

"I do, too," Sheryl said, moving closer to him. "I'm so scared I'm shaking. My goose bumps have goose bumps on them."

"Sure they do."

"They do," she stated. "Do you want to see?"

241

"Uh-uh. Not now. There's a bunch of real goose bumps on the cliff I want to watch."

"Very funny," the girl muttered, grinning in spite of herself. "Very, very funny. I almost . . . Jase, look!"

Jason, caught up in the drama on the top of the cliff, forgot for the moment that he was standing next to the most beautiful girl in all the world. He forgot that he liked her; he forgot that she liked him; he forgot that she made him nervous; he forgot everything but the fact that a goose named Chester, a goose who had once saved his life, was plunging off the cliff above him.

"I see him!" he shouted excitedly. "There he goes, over the edge! Oh, no! Chester, don't fall! Come on! Come on! Fly, you big dumb bird! Fly!"

"Jase," Sheryl cried, unconsciously grabbing the boy's arm in her own anxiety, "he's falling! Look, he isn't . . . Oh, no! His wings are out, but he's still falling. Why isn't he slowing down? Oh, Jason, this is awful! I can't bear to watch!"

"Do it, Chester!" Jason shouted, his hands clenched before him. "Do it! Flap those wings! Harder, harder! Come on!"

And so, while Jason and Sheryl watched in fear, the gray form of the Canadian goose plummeted toward the bottom of the Petticoat Cliffs. His wings were indeed spread, and he was even beating them up and down, up and down. But still he fell, almost straight down, dropping rapidly toward certain death.

Jason stared transfixed, the horror of the moment filling his heart, while Sheryl dropped her eyes and, choking back a sob, covered her face with her hands.

But then, when it seemed that there was no time left for anything to change, something did. Chester, somehow, was not falling quite so fast. Besides, his wings were beating more rapidly, his long neck was stretched out . . .

"Sheryl!" Jason screamed as he grabbed the girl's trembling hand in his own. "Look! I think, I think . . ."

And as the two stared upward, the big goose's descent slowed, he beat noisily against the rushing air beneath his body, and suddenly, gracefully, he was flying, swooping low over their heads, straining upward, lifting, circling, flying—

"He's doing it!" Jason shouted as he reached unthinkingly for an equally exuberant Sheryl. "He's flying! He really is! I can't believe it!"

And then, without even realizing quite how it had happened, Jason found his arms around Sheryl. Even more amazing was the fact that her arms were around him as well, and her upturned face was directly before his own.

For an instant that lasted almost forever he watched as her eyes, her soft and lovely eyes, slowly closed, and he noticed then how her unbelievably long lashes were pressed against her cheeks, almost as if she were asleep. Only she wasn't, not at all. He could tell by the gentle but insistent pressure against the back of his neck, pressure that pulled him closer to her, closer, closer; and suddenly her lips were touching his own and the world was incredibly wonderful and the feeling was incredibly indescribable and Chester, flying above them, was somehow forgotten almost entirely . . .

And after a few seconds that seemed an eternity (or maybe it was the other way around) they separated and looked at each other. Both of them were exhilarated because Chester was flying and Jason, suddenly realizing what had happened, was exhilarated and mortified for other reasons. Quickly he dropped his arms and turned away before Sheryl could see the red creep up his face and fill his ears. He wanted somehow to tell her how thankful he felt about Chester *and* her, but he didn't know how to begin, and he was worrying and wondering, too, about how he had ever dared to do such a thing as to kiss her in the first place . . .

And so he never did see the pure but knowing smile that played across the lips of the more than beautiful Sheryl Hanson as she looked from him to the high-flying goose and back to him again, the pretty little smile that told the world she knew exactly how he felt about gratitude, and told the world also that she knew exactly how the kiss had happened. And furthermore that she fully intended, one day soon, to see that it happened again because, very simply, she really did like this boy called Jason Tilby who was so well on his way to becoming a fine and wonderful man, the kind of man she knew she would be interested in becoming interested in forever.

And meanwhile, high above them, circling now over two excited and shouting younger brothers, a single goose who had only one leg lifted and thrust downward with his huge wings and maneuvered his primary feathers and flew, really flew. And the two brothers, who were shouting and yelling for Chester to leave, wept openly, not caring at all who saw, because both were filled with the same grateful sense of final, ultimate success.

And thus, while the two boys above and the young couple below stared tearfully upward, Chester soared higher, made a sharp bank against the late glowing sky which was quickly lowering with cloud, and gracefully beat his way away, moving back in the general direction of the Tilby home, moving at last toward the long-dreamed-of South.

Chapter 28
Travis Senses the Truth

When the boys got home that night, it was dark and cold and threatening snow, but that didn't dampen their spirits. Travis and Chester and Jenni and Jason and Steven and Sheryl had won, and nothing could change that, not even the season and old Mr. Larson.

"Mom and Dad," Travis shouted excitedly as he banged through the kitchen door, "he did it! Chester really flew! We won!"

No one responded immediately, and Travis was suddenly confused. While his two older brothers filed into the silent room, he looked more closely at his parents, who were gazing somberly at him.

"Mom?" he questioned. "Dad? Didn't you hear me? Chester flew, and now Mr. Larson can't have him."

"We know, son," Hank replied quietly. "We're glad that he finally flew."

"Yeah," Trav grinned, finally relaxing. "He did. Man, was it great, too. There was Chester, up against those clouds, soaring . . . Wait a minute. How did you know? We just got here."

Lois stood up and walked to her son and took him in her arms. "Chester came home almost an hour ago, Trav. Jenni's been trying to make him go away again ever since, but he won't. He refuses to fly."

"No!" Travis screamed. *"No!* He can't stay! I won't let him!"

"You have no choice, son," Hank counseled. "He'll never leave, no matter what we do. You love him and he loves you, and he'll stick with you as long as he lives. That's the way geese are."

"But, Dad," Travis wailed in anguish, "he can't. Doesn't he know what tomorrow is?"

"I doubt it. But even if he did I don't think he'd go. He loves you too much. Some fine creatures, and a few very great men and women, place love and loyalty above even life itself. I'd say we've been pretty lucky to have such a goose in our family this past summer. Wouldn't you?"

Travis nodded slowly, and then he looked up. "Does . . . does that mean tomorrow I've got to . . . to . . ."

Hank nodded, and Travis, his face reflecting the intense grief in his heart, suddenly broke from his mother's grasp and fled outside. Hank started to follow, but Lois reached and touched his arm, stopping him.

"Let him be alone," she suggested quietly. "He needs to work this out with Chester and himself."

Hank looked bleakly at his wife. "I guess you're right," he said as he turned slowly away. "It's awfully hard, though. If I could only feel right about it, I'd do this for him. I'd do it in a minute. I can hardly stand to see him hurting."

Lois buried her face in her husband's shirt, her emotions overcoming her. "I . . . I know," she replied as she sobbed silently into the strength of his embrace. "Oh, *how* I know!"

Jason and Steve, sensing that their folks needed to be alone as much as Travis did, turned and walked outside together. Over by the pens they could see Travis, who was throwing Chester into the air again and again, sobbing and yelling at him to go, to get out of his life.

"Sure tough, isn't it?" Jason said after they were off the porch.

"Yeah, I'll say," Steve agreed. "It's rotten."

"Isn't it, though? I just wish it had worked."

"So do I. It's kind of funny, isn't it? You don't want to help and you feel guilty, so you repent and want to help; and it turns out there's really nothing you can do, anyway."

Jason smiled slightly in the darkness, feeling suddenly close to his younger brother. "Oh, I don't know," he said gently. "I think you did a whole lot."

"Yeah, maybe. But not tonight. Tonight there's nothing either of us can do!"

"Not for Travis, I guess," Jason agreed. "But we can sure help Mom and Dad. I'll go milk Gerty. You start on the other chores if you'd like, and I'll help you as soon as I'm done."

"You've got a deal," Steve replied, grinning at his older brother. "Then when we're through, let's go see if we can help Trav. I mean, you never know. Maybe Chester'll fly yet."

Jason beamed at Steve, and then with their arms around each other's shoulders the two brothers headed for the corral.

Chapter 29
All Things Come . . .

"*Quiet!* All right, you kids," Coach Gruninger boomed. "Thanksgiving's coming up, the big vacation, so you oughta be ready. Who's going to be the first one to strain his fat little guts on this rope climb?"

It was Tuesday afternoon, last period, and Travis had never felt so discouraged. Chester was home waiting, and he was going to have to kill him in another hour or so.

Oh, he groaned inwardly, *why didn't he go? Why is it that he and I have to be such klutzes? Why couldn't one of us—*

And then Travis had an idea, a crazy illogical idea that made no sense at all. But . . . but maybe it did!

"Dear God," he whispered, "if I climb that rope, then . . ."

"Travis Tilby!" somebody shouted teasingly.

Everyone started to laugh, and even Coach, after he had made certain that Mrs. Anderson wasn't around, smiled, too. But suddenly there was silence, total and complete, for Travis Tilby was standing next to the rope.

"Trav," Steve called out, not even considering what his friends might think. "No!"

But Travis, ignoring his older brother, spoke only to the coach. "This is for you, sir. You'll need your stopwatch, and I want a countdown so I'll know when to start."

For a brief moment the coach hesitated, unsure of what he dared do. But the kid was there, and he'd volunteered. No one could make anything more of that than was already there. So, grinning more widely than ever, Coach pulled out his watch and spoke.

"You betcha, Mr. Tilby. You betcha! Okay, kids . . . stand back. This boy's going for the record."

There were a few more laughs, but Travis stood silently, ignoring them. He was going to climb that rope for Chester! He was going to—

"Get ready!"

Never in his life had Travis been so certain of what he was going to do. He was scared to death, but he was going to—

"Get set!"

Chester, he thought as he sucked in his breath, *please know what I am doing. This is really for you, not Coach! If I can climb this dumb rope, then you can fly away! You—*

"Go!"

Travis had no memory of jumping or of catching

251

the rope. His first thought was the startled realization that he had just scrambled past the twelve-foot mark, his former high point. *My gosh*, he thought to himself, *I'm going to do it. I'm really going to . . .*

And then the pain and exhaustion hit his hands and arms like giant hammers, and he was sure he was going to fall. *No*, he cried out to himself. *No! Remember Chester! Remember that he has to—*

In Travis's mind he could see his goose, soaring into the sunset, banking, turning, gliding, beating his wings higher and higher, never giving up, never quitting.

Slowly the boy inched up the rope, straining, agonizing, his eyes squeezed shut against the pain in his arms and shoulders. *Up, lift the right hand up, grasp, pull, now the left hand, hold, squeeze, hold the rope with your feet, push, pull, strain, more—more—think of Chester—more—*

Travis could never remember such pain. He had been on the rope forever, and it stretched away forever upward. He was only a speck upon it, lost somewhere in the middle of eternity, pulling, straining and reaching, gasping against the agony in his chest, hands, and arms, doing his best to drown out the noise that flooded over him each time he managed to drag himself up another hand's width—

Noise?

Travis concentrated, and suddenly he was aware that the kids below him, the ones who had so eagerly made fun of him before, were—were chanting!

"Fifteen!"

He could hardly believe it. They were counting for him, cheering for him. Each time he grasped upward they yelled, telling him that he could do it, that they knew he could do it, that he was doing it, that he—

"Sixteen!"

"Seventeen!"

"Eighteen!"

The noise was deafening, but maybe it wasn't noise so much as it was the sound of blood rushing in Travis's ears. He had never felt such pressure, such pain, such—

"Nineteen!"

Was he really that close? His eyes were closed, so he couldn't see, but he knew it wasn't so. It couldn't possibly be. There was no way he could climb that high. Besides, he could go no farther, anyway. There was nothing left in him, no strength, no energy, no will—

"Twenty!"

Whap!

Somehow, though he knew it couldn't have happened, Travis's hand had smacked against something hard. Forcing his eyes open and looking up through a strange sort of red mist, he was surprised to see the beam there, directly above his head, around which the rope was tied. Then he knew and his heart soared and he smacked the beam again and he was sliding down the rope and the noise was unbelievable and the applause was deafening and he was on the floor and standing, his whole body shaking, looking up at Coach Gruninger.

"Wh . . . what was m . . . my time?" he asked breathlessly as Coach simply stared at him.

The cheering continued unabated and Coach, totally dumbfounded, at last held up his hand for silence. Then, as the crowd grew still, he gaped first at his watch and then again at Travis. "You *did* it," he replied, his voice filled with awe. "I can't believe you did it."

"Not m . . . me alone, Coach," the boy replied, still gasping for breath. "It was me and Ch . . . Chester."

"What? Who? But I don't . . ."

"N . . . never mind. Just t . . . tell me my t . . . time."

"Uh . . . one minute eighteen seconds. It was pretty slow, but you did it, young Mr. Tilby. You *did* it! If you keep practicing, with that kind of determination you'll beat everybody here."

"I . . . I don't need to," Travis replied quietly. "I'm not competing against them. I hope everyone here does better than I just did. But record my time, Coach, because it *was* a record—mine! Write it down, because before June I'll beat it all hollow. Between now and then I'll be getting better than me every day."

And then, while Coach stared in amazed and probably confused silence, Travis picked up his coat, grinned at Steve—who grinned and winked proudly back—and then, while his classmates cheered again, the young man walked confidently out of the room, ready at last to have his goose fly away.

Chapter 30
The Ultimate Sacrifice

It was snowing, and Travis, his heart filled with fear, was sitting in the old barn with Chester. He had tried to the best of his ability, he really had, but nothing had happened, nothing had worked! Chester, even after his prayer and his rope climb, still refused to fly, to leave.

"Like I told Jenni," he finally murmured as he stroked Chester's feathers, "it's just my luck. My lousy rotten crummy luck!"

For a few moments more he sat still, staring ahead, feeling but doing his best not to think. Then the sound of a distant car horn turned his mind on, he thought of old Mr. Larson, and suddenly his stomach filled once more with pain.

"Chester," he whispered, his face reflecting his agony, "what are we going to do? Mr. Larson's coming to get you, and I don't know how to stop him! I have to, I know that. Only . . . I . . . I can't!"

Again Travis was silent, wiping a new batch of tears from his eyes. Chester, as though nothing was wrong, was doing his best to get his bill filled with one of the boy's ears; and Travis could hardly stand the bird's flippant happiness.

"Come on, you dumb goose," the boy grumbled. "Stop playing around. Don't you know you're going to die, and I can't even think of a way to save you! Now, stop it and let me think!"

And then, as Chester pulled back his head and locked his soft black eyes on to Travis, as if he were asking the boy what was wrong, Travis started once again to cry. Chester, seemingly worried about his friend, lay his head down upon the boy's shoulder, and then softly began clicking out his love.

Travis, unable to stand any more, sobbed as if his heart would break; and burying his face in the feathered softness of Chester's body, he held the goose close and poured out his agony.

"Oh, Chester," he sobbed quietly. "You *can't* die. You just *can't*! I love you too much!"

Again there was silence—silence broken only by Chester's soft clicking and Travis's muffled sobs. And so, now saying good-bye, they remained a very small pair of God's special creatures who had somehow found each other along the lonely pathway of life and who had also been blessed to find the doorway that led them into each other's hearts.

A little later when Hank and Lois came quietly into the barn, Travis was still there, still sitting in the cold, moldy hay and still holding Chester tightly in his arms.

Silently they sat down beside him. Lois put her

arms around this small and vulnerable son of hers, and then gently she began singing, something she had not done for Travis in years. Hank, moved as much as was his wife, reached out and gently caressed Chester's head and long silky neck.

"Trav," Hank finally said, "Mr. Larson called. He wants to pick up his goose this afternoon."

"Dad!" Travis wailed. "No! He can't! You can't let him! Please?"

"Honey," Lois whispered brokenly as she held her son even more closely, "we know what you're feeling, and we're so sorry. If there was anything we could do . . ."

"But there is!" Travis pleaded. "Stop him! Tell him he can't have him."

"Trav," Hank said gently, "Chester *is* Mr. Larson's, you took his money to raise the goose, and *you* made the deal with him. That was a commitment, son."

"But, Dad, I didn't know all this would happen! I didn't know—"

"Sweetheart," Lois said, gently interrupting her son, "your father is right, and deep inside you know it. You're too fine a boy to think otherwise. And of course you didn't know. None of us know as we go through life what is going to happen, but we go, anyway, trusting that one day God will make everything right. If you had known that this was going to happen, would you have chosen not to have Chester, not to feel his love?"

Slowly Travis shook his head back and forth.

"Of course you wouldn't," Lois continued. "Why, we've had seven glorious months with Chester,

257

and that's more than anyone else in the whole world will have with him. Ever! Just think how blessed we are."

"You know, Trav," Hank continued, "Chester's been a very wonderful part of our family. But listen to me for a minute. It isn't easy to watch someone that we love, die. Nevertheless, the Lord—"

"Wait a minute," Travis cried, almost shouting. "Why didn't God stop this? You said to pray, and all of us have been praying all summer. Why didn't God help Chester want to fly away?"

"Travis," Hank replied, doing his best to hold back his own tears as he watched his son's agony, "I don't know that we can tell you why. Maybe there isn't a reason. However, I really believe there is. It's just that we don't know it yet."

"But, Dad, God didn't even answer our prayers."

"Yes he did, son. He just said no. That means that somewhere in this there will be blessings for both you and your goose."

"And, honey," his mother added gently, "maybe this is how your prayer to let Chester fly *will* be answered. Can you think of a better place to fly than in heaven?"

"But . . . but I *love* him!"

"We all do, Trav. He's the most wondrously special pet we've ever had. All of us are going to miss him terribly. Still, it's time for him to go, and we all know it."

In the silence that followed, Travis hugged the goose to him once more, and once more he felt the soft head on his shoulder and heard the gentle clicking that told him he was loved.

"I just don't understand it," the boy finally said, speaking almost to himself. "Somehow it doesn't make sense."

"What doesn't?" Lois asked.

"All of this!" Travis declared bitterly. "Why did we try so hard? Why did *Chester* try so hard? If he's gonna die, anyway, what's the point of working like a fool to learn how to fly?"

Hank and Lois looked at each other for a moment, and then Hank reached out, took Travis's chin in his hand, lifted it, and looked his youngest son in the eyes.

"Son," he said gently, "do you remember how we've talked about opposition?"

Slowly Travis nodded.

"Good. Now, remember this as if a bronze plaque were fastened to your brain. The measure of a man's life is in how well he strives to overcome his personal handicaps, his God-allowed opposition. Neither his temporary failures nor life's unfair reversals or tragedies, and especially not his death, however untimely it seems, negates the value of his personal triumphs. They will go on forever— for him, for those who love him, and for all who follow after."

In the silence that followed, Travis held his goose and looked deeply into the bird's eyes while Hank and Lois looked on. The breath of each hung in frosty clouds in the still air of the old barn, and the whisper of the falling snow could be heard from outside.

"Dad's right, Chester," the boy finally declared. "You *flew*, and nothing's *ever* going to take that away from you. Besides that, you *cared*! You really did. You're the greatest friend that ever lived!"

"Travis," Hank finally said after his son had hugged the goose once again, "Mr. Larson will expect us to have his goose killed and prepared for him, just like we do the muttons. I've taken the axe out to the block, and if you'd like me to, I'll do it."

For a long moment Travis sobbed quietly, his face still buried against the warm breast of his goose. But at last, taking a deep breath, he lifted his head and wiped at his eyes.

"Th-thanks, Dad," he whispered. "But no. I . . . I guess I'd better do it."

"But why?" Lois asked quickly, her heart in her throat.

"Mom," Travis answered slowly, "it's part of the deal. Besides, if I do it, maybe Chester won't be so scared."

And so, while Hank and Lois Tilby watched their young son who had so suddenly been forced to grow up, Travis stood, placed Chester on the ground to follow, turned, and walked slowly out of the barn.

Immediately outside, however, the boy was startled to find Jason and Sheryl and Steve and Jenni standing quietly together, waiting for him.

Saying nothing, Steve dropped to his knees, threw his arms around Chester, and squeezed. Jason and Sheryl then did the same, and last of all, so did Jenni.

"Chester," she said tearfully as the goose laid his head gently into her small cold hands, "Chester, I love you so awful much, even better than a thousand trillion gooses. I hope you're happy up in heaven."

For a moment then they all stood grouped together, their arms around each other and their tears of love and unity flowing freely. And while they stood, hoping for the one miracle that wasn't coming, Chester hopped back and forth from one to the other, the old enmities long forgotten, his love a constant and contagious thing, hissing and clicking quietly and acting for all the world like he was saying good-bye and telling them to be happy because he'd see them again one day soon.

"Say," Hank suddenly said as he realized what Chester was saying, "do you remember the day Chester chased old Gerty so much that she tried to climb up into the apple tree?"

There were sudden snickers among the sniffles; and then Lois, understanding what her husband was doing, brought back a memory herself.

"I do," she declared. "The day I'll never forget, though, was the day Chester attacked poor Mrs. Sudsup at church."

There were more snickers than sniffles, and for the next few minutes the Tilbys and Sheryl talked of nothing but Chester, remembering him, laughing at him, loving him, seeing him in their minds, building such a picture of him that it seemed almost as if Chester had nothing to do with the softly clicking mound of flesh and feathers that was hopping around among them.

Finally, when Hank was quite sure that none of them were leaving Chester behind in the orchard

261

but instead were taking him with them in their minds and memories and hearts, he put his arm around Travis and signaled gently that it was time to go.

Travis looked up at his father, took a deep breath, wiped his face with the sleeve of his coat, and turned his reluctant steps toward the old chopping block down in the orchard.

"Come on, Chester," he said softly as he lifted the big goose into his arms. "It's . . . it's time for you to . . . to fly away forever."

And then together the two of them walked slowly away.

Chapter 31
Chester Is Gone

As the boy and the goose disappeared into the trees, the sound of Mr. Larson's pickup pulling into their driveway caught the attention of the rest of the family. Hurriedly they made their way back to the house; and while Hank began speaking quietly with Mr. Larson, who by then was out of his pickup, the remainder of the family went inside to wait.

Lois furiously attacked a sink full of dirty dishes, Jason and Steve and Sheryl furiously attacked their studies, and little Jenni, who was weeping openly, climbed onto the couch and stared out the window at the desolate-looking orchard.

The early winter snow was falling harder, covering the ground, and Jenni rubbed first her eyes and then the window, wiping off the steam her warm breath had created, trying to see the orchard, wanting to see when her brother at last came out. She knew he was hurting, and she ached for him and for Chester, wishing with all her heart that she had been older so she could have helped more.

Suddenly she rubbed her eyes, and then she rubbed them again. "Mom," she called anxiously, "Mr. Larson's gone into the orchard."

Lois looked out the window above the sink, and instantly she knew that something was wrong. She had seen Mr. Larson talking with Hank, and now he was running through the trees—actually running.

Without even drying her hands she bolted through the door and into the yard, and the other Tilbys, seeing her leave, hastily followed.

Travis, standing alone in a clearing with his goose, stared fearfully at the chopping block. Chester, totally unconcerned, hopped forward and fluttered clumsily up onto the stump, where he stood, clicking softly at the boy. Angrily Travis lifted the axe and slammed it into the snow.

"I don't want to do this to you, Chester. I just don't . . ."

And then the words stuck in his throat. As more tears came, Travis sobbed his loneliness and grief.

"You stupid bird!" he yelled at the still clicking goose. "Why did you have to come back? You flew away. Why didn't you just *stay* away? That was a real stupid move, you know that?"

Frustrated, Travis spun about and tromped back to the stump, where he plopped down, his back to the bird, weeping openly.

"You know I love you, Chester. We've had some really good times, you and me, and you've helped me a lot, you know that? I never would have climbed that rope if it hadn't of been for you. I never could have stood up against Coach ... or Alec, either, for that matter."

Taking a deep breath, Travis took hold of Chester's head and pulled him close.

"We've had the summer of our lives, Chester," he sobbed, wiping away his tear-stained cheeks. "And I just want to say thanks. I am always going to remember you, I promise ..."

Sniffing back more tears, Travis pushed Chester from him, stood up, and reached for the axe.

Still clicking, Chester, almost knowingly, stretched his neck across the chopping block toward Travis.

Stroking the goose's feathered head affectionately, Travis did his best to smile. Then, with gentle firmness, he applied more pressure, holding the neck in place against the wooden stump.

"I ... I promise ..."

Chester struggled against Travis's grip, but with a tear-stained grimace, Travis held him hard. Then with his free hand, he pulled the axe from behind the stump and swung it into the air.

Suddenly from behind, something grabbed hold of the descending axe. Surprised, Travis released the goose and spun around, where he found himself staring into the serious and emotion-filled face of Mr. Larson.

"You're quite a man, Travis," Mr. Larson said, choking back his own tears. "Now, take that goose of yours and get on back to the house. I figure you've earned your money already."

"But . . . but . . ." Travis stammered, unable to comprehend what was happening.

"You don't have to talk, Travis, except for answering me one question."

Travis held his breath, afraid of what Mr. Larson was going to ask.

"The question is," the old man continued, "what in the arid land-o'-Goshen do you think my wife and I ought to eat for Thanksgiving dinner?"

And then the old man's face crinkled, and he smiled.

THANKSGIVING
DAY

Chapter 32
What a Day!

Well, by now you've no doubt figured out that it's me, Travis, who's been telling this story, and I want you to know that I've been holding fairly close to the way things really were. And, outside of a couple of minor details, I don't have much left to say. Those two or three things should be mentioned, however, so let's get at it.

First, that was far and away the best Thanksgiving dinner I've ever had, before or since. Dad moved the big old table into the living room, and then while Steve set it with Mom's best china and silver, Dad and Jenni decorated the walls with pictures of Pilgrims and other things they thought we all ought to be thankful for. I even got out one of my drawings of Chester, and Dad and Jen hung it in the place of honor right next to the Pilgrims. That made me feel pretty darn good.

Meanwhile Mom kept Jase and me busy helping

her in the kitchen, and take my word for it, that was a *meal* she prepared! There were mashed potatoes and both brown and white gravy; there were yams; carrots; peas in white sauce; corn, both cut up and on the cob; and broccoli and cauliflower in more white sauce. There were salads like I've never seen before; there was cranberry sauce; turkey and dressing; and both brown and white fresh hot rolls smothered in our own homemade butter. There were milk and punch, and Dad even got out a few bottles of his home-brewed root beer. There were all kinds of fruit, both preserved and fresh; and in all the little spaces on the table where nothing else would fit, Mom squeezed in dishes of pickles and relishes and jams and jellies and applesauce.

I'll tell you, it was a feast! But the best part of all was what graced the huge platter in the center of the table. Frankly I've never eaten such a tasty tender juicy ham!

Mrs. Sudsup told us she hadn't ever eaten a better meal, either, and I believe that. Why? you ask. Because I sat across from her that day, and I've never seen anybody eat as much as she did. That is, I haven't unless I count old Mr. Larson and his wife. They sat next to me; and let me tell you, they really tanked down the goodies. Both of them! But then, so did Jason and Steve and I. Like I said, that was probably the finest Thanksgiving dinner I ever had, and it came in the middle of one of the finest days I ever lived.

And you know, when Dad finished asking a blessing on all the food, and thanking the Lord that Chester had been able to bless our lives, the loudest amen of all came from old Mr. Larson, who winked at me when I looked up at him. Yes, sir, it surely was a day of thanksgiving!

The best part of all, though, came just as Mom was dishing up dessert. I was just reaching for my slice of pumpkin pie when Chester's wild honking halted all conversation at the table.

"What on earth is that noise?" Mrs. Sudsup asked.

"It's Chester," I yelped, pushing back from the table. "Something's wrong."

Bursting through the back door, I could see Chester running back and forth across Mrs. Sudsup's yard. But I couldn't see anything wrong. Suddenly Mr. Larson, who had come out of the house behind me, put his hand upon my shoulder and pointed upward. Quickly I looked, and there, winging southward, was a long triangle of wild Canadian geese.

"Maybe you weren't meant to have Chester after all," Mr. Larson said quietly.

I didn't answer. Instead, I just stood, wide-eyed, as Chester honked again. Then, with a furious clicking and flapping of his wings, Chester ran across the yard, stretched his neck, broadened his wings, and almost as if he were in slow motion, he lifted into the sky.

In total disbelief I stared! Chester was flying! He had actually taken off by himself, and now he was lifting skyward, striving to reach the rapidly departing gaggle of wild geese.

"I knew you could do it, Chester," I whispered through new but happy tears. "I knew it all the time!"

*   *   *

"Steve," I heard Jason whisper later that night after the guests had gone home and the family had finally retired. "You awake?"

"Yeah," my next oldest brother mumbled sleepily from his bed, "what's wrong?"

"It's Trav. He's gone. His bed's empty."

"But where . . . ?"

"Hey, you guys," I whispered, careful so's my voice wouldn't carry outside of the room. "Come here, quick!"

"Trav," Jason called, "where are you?"

"I'm at the window," I whispered urgently, for once forgetting to try to make my voice deep like Steve's. "Hurry! If you don't, you'll miss them."

Stumbling out of bed, my two older brothers groped their way toward where I stood, staring upward.

"What?" Jason asked. "What is it?"

"There, up above those trees."

Well, they tried, straining to see past my outstretched finger. They really tried, but they couldn't see them. Because of the darkness or bleary eyes or one thing or another, they couldn't see; and so now, even after all these years, I occasionally find myself wondering. But I don't, really, for I know. I saw!

That night, unable to sleep, I stood alone at my bedroom window remembering Chester and the rope climb and feeling good and bad all at the same time from thinking about it and missing him; and suddenly I saw, beating their way southward, an irregular "V" formation of wild Canadian geese.

They were low, very low, and close, so close that I could see them distinctly. Of course they weren't the bunch Chester had flown off with. I knew that then, and I know it now. Still, he was there, as real as can be, just as he's been in every flock of Canadian geese I've ever seen since. And always he's as big as life, flying proudly, holding his real foot and his artificial one close against his body, showing off for me just like he did that summer when he and I and my family found out, finally, what it meant to belong to each other and all the rest of those we love, forever. And after all, isn't that how long memories last?

AUTHORS' NOTE

Though much of the preceding story is fictional, there was actually a Canadian goose whose name was Chester. He came into Blaine's life the summer he was thirteen, and made such an impact upon Blaine and his brother Brenton that neither they nor any other members of their family have ever forgotten him.

Chester was exactly as he was described in the story. He had only one foot, was basically a one-boy goose (unless Blaine was away), never learned to fly despite the intense efforts of Blaine and Brent and his brothers; was nearly always in trouble; and was nearly always getting Blaine and frequently the other Yorgason boys into trouble as well. And, like Travis in the story, Blaine had to struggle with the destiny of his pet when Thanksgiving came that year.

BLACKSTONE'S MAGIC ADVENTURES!

Use your wits and Blackstone's tricks to save the day!

☐ 56251-8   BLACKSTONE'S MAGIC ADVENTURE #1:
                 THE CASE OF THE MUMMY'S TOMB $1.95
☐ 56252-6   Canada $2.50

☐ 56253-4   BLACKSTONE'S MAGIC ADVENTURE #2
                 THE CASE OF THE GENTLEMAN GHOST $1.95
☐ 56254-2   Canada $2.50

☐ 56255-0   BLACKSTONE'S MAGIC ADVENTURE #3
                 THE CASE OF THE PHANTOM TREASURE $1.95
☐ 56256-9   Canada $2.50

Buy them at your local bookstore or use this handy coupon:
Clip and mail this page with your order

TOR BOOKS—Reader Service Dept.
49 W. 24 Street, 9th Floor, New York, NY 10010

Please send me the book(s) I have checked above. I am enclosing
$_____ (please add $1.00 to cover postage and handling).
Send check or money order only—no cash or C.O.D.'s.

Mr./Mrs./Miss _____
Address _____
City _____ State/Zip _____
Please allow six weeks for delivery. Prices subject to change without
notice.

ZORK
A WHAT-DO-I-DO-NOW BOOK

☐ 57975-5   ZORK #1: THE FORCES OF KRILL $1.95
   57976-3   Canada $2.50

☐ 57980-1   ZORK #2: THE MALIFESTRO QUEST $1.95
   57981-X   Canada $2.50

☐ 57985-2   ZORK #3: THE CAVERN OF DOOM $1.95
   57986-0   Canada $2.50

☐ 55989-4   ZORK #4: CONQUEST AT QUENDOR $1.95
   55990-8   Canada $2.50

Buy them at your local bookstore or use this handy coupon:
Clip and mail this page with your order

TOR BOOKS—Reader Service Dept.
49 W. 24 Street, 9th Floor, New York, NY 10010

Please send me the book(s) I have checked above. I am enclosing
$_____ (please add $1.00 to cover postage and handling).
Send check or money order only—no cash or C.O.D.'s.

Mr./Mrs./Miss _____

Address _____

City _____ State/Zip _____

Please allow six weeks for delivery. Prices subject to change without
notice.